GUARDED

GUARDED

KIRSTEN LASINSKI

MOODY PUBLISHERS
CHICAGO

Library of Congress Cataloging-in-Publication Data

Lasinski, Kirsten.
  Guarded / Kirsten Lasinski.
     p. cm.
  ISBN-13: 978-0-8024-5568-0
     1. Adoptees—Fiction. 2. Divorced women—Fictiion.
  3. Mothers and daughters—Fiction. 4. Colorado—Fiction. I. Title.

PS3612.A84G83 2005
813'.6—dc22

                                                  2004027352

                  ISBN: 0-8024-5568-9
            EAN/ISBN-13: 978-0-8024-5568-0

              1 3 5 7 9 10 8 6 4 2

         Printed in the United States of America

ONE

EMILY tore through the trees. She choked back a sob as she barreled up the hillside, digging for handholds in the sandy soil of the mountain.

"Stupid!" She swore. "How could I be so stupid?"

The soil gave way to boulders pocked with lichen and slopes of broken shale that slipped beneath her feet as she climbed, and the landscape shifted before her eyes. Boulders hopped from one side of the path to the other as her vision wobbled in an airy wave of dizziness. Emily shook her head, fighting the symptoms she knew would only grow worse. It was inevitable, this trouble she was in. Maybe it always had been.

"Oh, God, what am I going to do?"

Her sneaker lodged beneath a root. She plunged forward, rocks digging at her palms as she splayed against the earth. Tears fell hot on her cheeks.

Just a little farther.

It was just a few more feet to utter solitude and the solace of her well-worn perch over the town. Just a few more feet.

"To oblivion," she whispered.

The thought released a cold wash into her veins.

It would be so easy to fling herself from the craggy cliff and end her misery, taking her unlucky burden along. Emily wiped her palms down her jeans. She was only eighteen, too young and too afraid to die. Besides, if there was a God, she didn't want to meet him in her current state.

A moan escaped her lips. What had she done? She felt regret hardening into a lump beneath her ribs.

"I don't even love him."

She wasn't even sure what the word *love* meant. And now they would be bound for life by their mistake. A tear snaked a path down the side of her nose.

What would her friends think? Thank God her mother wasn't alive to see her joke of a daughter screw up again. What would her father say? She was too old for the back of his hand, but not for his cutting remarks. Not for his calculated distance or curt advice, she thought, and tasted a strange, new bitterness. He always knew how to put her on the outside.

Emily grasped at a tree and hauled herself up, sinking her fingers into the soft knots of sap along the trunk. The piercing fragrance plucked more tears from her eyes as she wiggled her hand free, leaving smeared fingerprints in the sticky bulbs.

How ironic.

The marks were tiny monuments to her miserable life. The only evidence that she really existed, and no one could even read them.

"I feel like I don't even know who I am."

I never have.

Swaying in the shadow of the ragged fir, Emily was suddenly afraid.

"Oh, God," she whispered, "what have I done?"

TWO

A SOFT, moody dusk pressed through the trees as Emily Blyton turned back toward the bridge. Stars punctured the eastern sky, multiplying in a glory undimmed by city lights.

"There's no place like home," she sighed.

Running to the neighbor's for a cup of sugar took a little longer in the rugged terrain of Murray, Colorado, than in most places, but a warm sense of community persisted nonetheless. Who would have guessed a century ago that the belly-up mining town named after the first crusty digger to strike silver there would one day be a bustling burg of tourism? A gem tucked into the craggy embrace of the Rockies, redolent with the breath of a million pines?

Emily exhaled as her boots hit the bridge. The trek to the Masons' was short, but steep and boulder-strewn. Hiking it alone that evening had earned Emily a lecture from Rebecca

"Bug" Mason, her dearest friend and Ian's sprightly wife, on the dangers of stumbling around the mountain in the dark.

"What if you got lost?" she'd asked, measuring sugar into gleaming Tupperware. "What if you broke your ankle on those rocks? I don't know if we'd hear you."

Emily nodded dutifully.

"Yes, Mother." She smiled.

Bug swatted her with a dish towel.

"I'm serious. Do I need to remind you of what happened to Harry?"

Ian groaned from the living room, where he lay stretched in his favorite recliner, pecking at his laptop.

"You don't believe that yarn about the mountain lion, do you?"

"Harry lost his leg in the war," Emily said. "He tells that story to frighten tourists. Plus, I think it makes him feel important. Defending our nation's freedom apparently wasn't enough."

"Ahh," Bug nodded. "The Blyton sarcasm makes its nightly appearance."

Emily frowned. "I'm not that bad, am I?"

"Only in the evenings, dear."

Bug handed her the sugar and a flashlight, which flickered and died halfway down the hill. Poor Ian, he was just too busy to keep track of such mundane details as flashlight maintenance. What with that bustling church and all.

The novelty of Ian Mason as a preacher never wore off for Emily. Ian, who gave her battered Bronco a tune-up every six months, whether it needed it or not, who cleaned house at the monthly poker games in Town Hall and drove neighbors home from parties without a word of reproach after they'd had too much to drink, who never spoke a word of gossip about any-one despite knowing the dirt on practically everyone.

Bug was no better. What kind of preacher's wife sold Tup-perware and cosmetics, and made at killing at both? What kind of preacher's wife drove a Harley around town, without a helmet?

Nine years later, Emily still blushed at the memory of how she and Ian had met. She had been stuck beneath her car for the better part of an hour, her oil pan tottering in one hand while its contents dripped onto her face, when Ian rode up on his mountain bike. Emily saw the nubby tires pull up beside her just as she finished swearing loudly at the car.

Ian's cheerful face appeared upside-down beside her front bumper and offered to help. Left with little other choice, she thanked him profusely and ducked into the house to wipe the grime from her face and scrounge at the back of her fridge for the solitary bottle of beer she kept for such an occasion. After changing her oil with the ease of a seasoned mechanic and politely declining the beer, Ian introduced himself as the pas-tor of the new church in town. Emily could still remember the sensation of blood rushing up her neck to her face as she fran-tically reviewed every inappropriate comment she had made in the last twenty minutes. In a horrified act of penance, she had promised to visit his church, but as Sunday rolled past drowsy Sunday, her chagrin was forgotten in the woods along with her promise, ground into the forest floor like the season's withered leaves.

Maybe it was the dim memories from her childhood of velvet railings, oppressive organ tunes, and whispered admo-nitions to *stop squirming,* but she couldn't bear the thought of going back to church. Maybe she was just afraid of what she'd find. Would Bug look down at the parishioners from a nose grown suddenly pinched and pious? Would Ian perch in a lofty pulpit set apart from the rustling crowd? Would he wear a robe? She laughed, then shivered at the thought. Someday she would try church, she supposed. She just hadn't been that desperate yet.

A warm, wet nose puffed at the screen door of her cabin home.

"Moscow, you silly boy." The Irish setter fanned his tail as she stroked his head. "I was only gone for an hour."

She changed the batteries in the flashlight for Ian, kicked her boots into the closet, and turned her attention back to the cookies she had promised to bring to the library's bake sale.

Ugh.

Her reflection grimaced in the dark window over the sink as she poured in the sugar and mixed, grinding at the stiff dough with a wooden spoon.

I look so old.

She tucked a lock of wheat-colored hair behind her ear, wishing she could forget about her birthday next month. Why was turning forty-one so much harder than turning forty? Forty hadn't fazed her. She was healthy and attractive and well-liked by her many friends and neighbors, she had reasoned last year, so what else mattered?

"I have an ex-husband I haven't spoken to in ten years," her reflection mumbled. "I have a twenty-three-year-old daughter who lives on the opposite side of the country and hardly speaks to me. I have no living relatives I care to talk to. Both my parents are dead."

Visions of her father's funeral pressed in on her as she spooned the cookies onto a pan: a persistent drizzle slicking the coffin, a creeping sense of loss, the pang of guilt when she couldn't cry. Had it been two years already? What was it he had tried to tell her, groping weakly at her arm before he died?

The oven timer rang, sending Emily out of her skin. Moscow barked.

"It's OK, boy," she gasped. "I'm just a little jumpy tonight." She reached for an oven mitt and pulled the curtain over the window.

THREE

MOSCOW blew heavily through his nose and allowed his eyelids to droop for a moment. The heavy smell of Emily's soldering iron wafted over the dog, lulling him to sleep as he lounged on the gravel driveway, ignoring the twittering sparrows in the pines. In the shadows of the open garage, Emily carefully set the joints of a window frame before laying her iron in its cradle and pulling off her gloves. She stepped back from the bench to admire her work. It was one of the largest pieces she had ever made, a mammoth arc of leaded stained glass curved to sit above the mammoth doors of some millionaire's mammoth summerhouse.

"And he probably only stays there two weeks out of the year."

Unused summer homes and trendy tourists were so much a part of Murray that locals joked about having eight months of winter and four months of company, but Emily didn't mind the tourism. After all, the picture-snapping retirees and aloof socialites were what kept her in business. Designing custom stained-glass windows wasn't exactly an in-demand profession anywhere else, but it kept her thick with customers and never hurting for money in Murray. Jericho had suggested rather tersely in her last email that Emily have someone design a website for her so she could sell her artistic creations online. Then she wouldn't be so "limited by location," as Jericho put it. It wasn't a bad idea. Emily graciously replied that she would look into it, and asked her daughter how New York was treating her. Did she get the birthday present Emily had sent? There was no reply.

Emily sighed and sat down next to Moscow in the sun. Her relationship with her daughter had never been an easy one, but she thought they had been making progress before Jericho announced two summers ago that she was moving to New York.

"I need that artistic climate," she had said, waving a brush toward a spattered canvas, "if I'm ever going to sell some of these."

Emily had been supportive, understanding, and devastated.

"Why should the distance matter?" Jericho had demanded when Emily suggested that she was trying to put distance between them. "We'll be as close as we've always been."

Emily wasn't sure if the words were meant to comfort or pain her, but they gnawed nonetheless, worming a hole into her heart. Had she erred in raising her daughter? Sure, she hadn't come running every time Jericho fell, but that was to teach her, to help her grow strong.

"It worked," Emily mumbled, "too well."

Moscow puffed in agreement and rolled onto his side.

Emily wove her fingers through the soft fur of his belly,

staving off a wave of guilt that threatened to crush her. Jericho was still hurting, still wounded by her relationship with her father, or lack thereof.

That wasn't my fault.

Rick had married Emily when she was eighteen and pregnant and had stuck around for a while. That was better than some, she knew, but he was selfish and lazy, and in the end parenthood had proved too much for him. He'd left when Jericho was barely three and never looked back, and although Emily had tried to convince her daughter over the years that he wasn't such a terrible guy, the argument was thin, and Jericho was more than willing to see through it. She'd railed all through her tumultuous adolescence that Emily had driven him away, but eventually gave up and resigned herself to the lingering bitterness of abandonment.

Footsteps crunched up the driveway, sending Moscow into a fit of howls. Emily brushed herself off as she stood.

"Can I help you?"

The young postman looked up with a start from the bag slung across his torso, and Emily chided herself for sounding so abrupt. He pawed through the satchel, produced a piece of mail, and studied it.

"Are you Emily Blyton of seven-fifty-one Ptarmigan Drive?"

She nodded.

"Then this," he held out the long envelope, "is for you."

"Thank you."

She took it from him, absorbing him carefully. Dark hair, slightly longer than necessary, heavy black boots a contrast to the neat uniform, and an air of casual despondency would have made him the object of Jericho's affection, had she been there. She always seemed to gravitate to the edgier types, and

Emily couldn't help but wonder . . . was she seeing someone like that in New York?

He crunched back the way he came as Emily realized, too late, that she had been staring.

"Thank you." She waved the envelope and called after him, hoping she hadn't appeared rude. "Don't worry about the Dobermans next door. They're all talk."

He nodded and disappeared into a thicket of aspens. She patted Moscow distantly and turned the envelope over.

It didn't look like a bill. She slit the flap with a fingernail and pulled out a single sheet of paper and a small card inked in navy blue.

"Dear Ms. Blyton: Please find enclosed your new Social Security Card."

After multiple accidental washings and years of wear, her old card had finally succumbed with a resounding tear the last time she pulled it from her wallet. She'd been beginning to think that the new one would never arrive.

She fingered the cardstock with its fresh wash of blue and heard in a dim corner of memory the quiet scrape of her father's razor against his rough chin.

Sunlight streamed in from the south-facing windows of the small bedroom, gleaming on the wooden floors and enveloping her in a pocket of warmth. The clatter of breakfast and smell of bacon leaked in from the kitchen below. Emily bounced tentatively on the corner of her parents' bed, watching her father through the open bathroom door as he prepared for the day. She swung her dangling legs.

"What are you doing?"

"Shaving."

He navigated his Adam's apple with care, tapped the blade against the porcelain and toweled his face, buttoning a fresh shirt under his chin. Something fell to the floor as he gathered his wallet and watch from the bureau.

"What is that?"

"That's my driver's license."

He picked up the card and stuffed it into his wallet.

"What does it do?"

"It's an I.D.," he clipped. "It proves to people who I am."

She shut her lips around her next question. The familiar edge in his voice told her she was "working his last nerve." She seemed to do that a lot.

She slipped from the bed, giving him a wide berth as she left.

"He's a good man," she whispered in the hallway.

Everyone said so. Her mother said he was a good provider. Emily often saw him smiling with other people, and there was always someone near to shake his hand or clap him on the back. Why then was he like the neighbor's dog with her, growling when she came too near the fence? She had noticed something else as well. She lowered her head, praying he couldn't read her thoughts from the bedroom. He didn't hug her. In fact, he hardly touched her at all. Emily found a thread in her sleeve and wound her finger into it, tugging until her pinkie swelled. She would have to be better. Her finger flushed and began to pulse. She would have to try harder.

Moscow darted into the trees, hunting the elusive prey that filled his dreams with yelps and twitches. Emily jolted back to the present. She looked at the card again.

"I'm Emily Blyton," she whispered.

The phone trilled from inside. She jogged back to the house, lifting the receiver on the fourth ring.

"Hello? Oh, hi, Elsie, no, I'm fine, just out of breath . . . what's that? Oh, I was in the garage working on a project when the phone rang. No, Elsie, you're never an interruption. What's going on?"

Emily listened to the lengthy explanation, "mmm-ing" in the appropriate places. At sixty-seven years old, Elsie McLeod was still the head of both the Murray Public Library and the Murray Historical Society, which ran a tiny museum in town where tourists could soak up the Wild West aura of the once-booming mining camp. She was also known for her "excellent conversational skills," as Jericho used to giggle whenever Elsie called. Old Harry Heppner swore that he once started a conversation with her, put down the phone, ran to the post office, came home, and picked up the conversation where they left off, with Elsie none the wiser.

Still, there was a restfulness about Elsie that Emily envied. Maybe peace came with age, but Emily had hoped she would have figured it out by forty-one.

"I would love to help, Elsie. Anything for the museum. Public records? They store those in the basement, don't they?"

She scrawled the information on the back of a receipt.

"What's that? Yes, I'll be at the bake sale. See you soon."

She hung up and paused to catch her breath. The upcoming genealogy exhibit sounded like a fine idea. It would give locals a sense of pride and tourists something to gawk at other than the tacky trinkets sold in the shops along Main Street. But what had prompted Elsie to think of her for such a project? She didn't exactly have a fascinating family. Elsie said that the Historical Society was looking for a wide sampling of volunteers willing to research and map their genealogies for the museum, a "representative cross-section of Murray's residents."

"She probably asked me because she knows I have the time."

Emily sighed at the sound of her own voice. Was she destined to become one of those embittered old women, haggling over coupons in the grocery line? She wrestled down the dim loneliness that threatened to engulf her. She was a fool. She should be counting her many blessings, not whining over what she didn't have. Moscow climbed onto the couch with a furtive glance over his shoulder as Emily launched into a timeworn pep talk.

"I am healthy," she muttered. "I am financially secure. I am surrounded by friends and neighbors who care about me." She pulled a length of plastic wrap over a plate of cookies. "I have a daughter who . . . loves me. I am healthy." She started again as she piled the cookies into the back of the Bronco. "I am financially secure . . ."

The engine groaned twice and turned over, and Emily, still chanting her mantra, drove into town.

※

"Ms. Blyton!"

Happy voices clamored as Emily walked into the library. Story hour was almost over, and the children were squirming like fish pulled from the river. Emily joined them on the floor, hoping to quiet them by her example. The young woman with the book perched in her lap smiled her appreciation and turned the last page. Little hands reached for Emily, squeezing her arms and patting her hair and her back. A little boy climbed into her lap.

"Emmy," he whispered and patted her chin.

Emily fought a pang of longing as she held him close. When was the last time her daughter had willingly climbed into her arms? She remembered Jericho's small arms around her neck and her breath warm on her face.

"I miss Daddy," Jericho whimpered

"Me too, honey," Emily whispered. "Me too."

"Thanks."

Emily blinked. It was the story-hour girl, brushing a lock of brown hair from her warm brown eyes as the children scrambled up from the floor.

"Sometimes the kids get a little antsy toward the end."

"Tell me about it." Emily laughed a little too hard. "Last time I did story hour, I had to sit on a couple of them."

The girl thrust out her hand. She had a nice face, Emily thought, sweet and honest.

"I'm Helena Jantzen. I don't think I've met you yet."

Emily shook the offered hand, hoping that her own wasn't too cold. Elsie must have trolled the high school for volunteers recently.

"Emily. Emily Blyton. I thought I knew everyone in Murray."

"We just moved here from Miami."

"That explains the tan." Emily smiled and searched her mind for something else to say. It was like fumbling through a dark warehouse without a flashlight. "Florida is a far cry from Colorado. How did you end up here?"

Helena flinched as an involuntary flush stained her cheeks.

"My parents just divorced," she said, looking at her shoes. "My mom thought it would be good for us to have a change of scenery."

Emily nodded, feeling for the girl. She remembered the awful, leaden fear beneath her ribs at night when her father yelled, the dusty texture of antacids. While the other girls in junior high carried around breath mints and gum in the hopes of getting kissed, Emily carried Rolaids.

"I'm sorry. I know how messy divorces can get."

"Messy doesn't begin to describe it."

"Still, Murray is a rather random place to land." Emily tried to steer the conversation toward a less painful topic.

Helena smiled suddenly.

"Honestly, my mother just threw a dart at a map. It landed in Colorado between Murray and Vail. She chose Murray because she said she'd already been to Vail."

"I hope you have some of her adventurous spirit," Emily laughed.

Helena's smile turned coy.

"I'm having a good time so far. Murray's got a surprising number of cute guys for such a small town."

"If you see any cute forty-year-olds, send them my way."

"What's this?" Elsie appeared at their side, her volume rising with her pitch. "You looking for a man, Emily?"

Emily talked herself out of a blush and patted the older woman on the back.

"Always looking, Elsie, just not actively," she said. "Where do you want me to put these cookies?"

Elsie peeked beneath the foil.

"Let's set up a table outside," she suggested. "Underneath the awning in case it rains." She looked around the library with a sigh. "If we can get enough folks out here today, we'll finally be able to add that new wing. It's taken us five garage sales, two car washes, and three bake sales," she ticked the activities off on her fingers, "but it'll be worth it. Murray will finally have a real library."

Emily guessed by the dreamy look in Elsie's eyes that she

was imagining her name on a bronze plaque gracing the front of the new wing.

"Just let me know what I can do to help."

Elsie grunted. "You can get some of the old bachelors around here off of their lazy rears. Oh, they love my lemon bars when they're heaped in baskets at the church picnic, but do they come around when it's time for a bake sale? Noooo, they wouldn't part with a dime, even for a good cause. I'm only asking two-fifty for a whole plate! There must be three dozen bars here."

Emily bit her lip to keep from smiling as Elsie's tirade trailed off to a mutter.

"I've got nothing to do this afternoon," Helena offered. "I'd love to stay and help."

"Oh, bless the child," Elsie said. "You can man the cash box, dear. Goodness knows, your young mind is more apt with calculating change than mine. But don't give any samples to Cane McAllister." She wagged a plump index finger at Helena. "I don't care how old he is or how he begs, if he wants a lemon bar he's going to pay for it."

With that she toddled off, looking for hapless bystanders to recruit as volunteers. Helena looked at Emily.

"Who is Cane McAllister?"

"This is going to be a crash course for you in the who's who of Murray." Emily smiled. "Cane is one of our old-timers. He used to work the silver mines when Murray was little more than a tent colony. Word to the wise, don't ask him about the old country unless you've got an hour to kill."

"The old country?"

"Scotland."

"Ohh." Helena nodded. "The old country."

The three long tables they laid end-to-end were soon

groaning under the weight of cookies, brownies, bundt cakes, and bars, supplied by a small army of volunteers.

"Wow," Helena marveled. "This must be the small-town charm everyone talks about. I can't believe how many people contributed to this."

"More like Elsie's charm." Emily grinned. "If there's one thing she's truly gifted at, it's finding volunteers." She set a loaf of banana bread on the corner of a table. "Now we just need people to buy this stuff."

Within a few minutes, Helena was hard at work, taking money at the cash box as people drifted by, unable to resist the lure of the fluffy piles of macaroons and Elsie's fabled lemon bars. Emily noted with satisfaction that her cookies were among the first to go. She had secured her reputation as a decent cook and her name on Elsie's list of people to call.

"I'll be making cookies for Elsie till the day I die," she sighed.

Just then she noticed a crowd of tourists gathered beyond the bustle of the sale. What were they watching? Had someone fallen in the river again? An elderly gentleman in white shorts and a pastel polo clutched his sides and guffawed. Chuckles strayed into the sunshine of the August afternoon. Emily rose on her toes, straining to see above the heads, when she heard a familiar voice.

"I swear it's true, folks, that's what he told me."

Stanley Warwick. What is he up to now?

Stanley's voice sighed, melodic and smarmy as ever. "Yeah, Murray is a great place to live. Now, if I could just get a high-speed Internet connection, I'd be in heaven." More chuckles. "Enjoy your visit, folks, and be sure to stop by the store."

The crowd dispersed, making its way toward the bake sale

with bulging pockets and grumbling stomachs. Emily eased her way into the mob. Helena would need her help, and Stanley certainly didn't need her attention. Stanley Warwick owned two of the storefronts on Main Street: one that sold key chains, T-shirts with rainbow trout airbrushed across the chest, and chunks of fool's gold to tourists; and another that boasted popcorn, cotton candy, and an array of sickeningly sweet treats for gorging. Emily had gone out to dinner with him once, several years ago when he first arrived in Murray, and decided between the appetizer and the entrée that once was enough. He was handsome enough, in a balding sort of way, but Stanley was just too . . . Stanley.

"Thank goodness you're back," Helena whispered. "These people are crazy. You'd think they'd never seen a chocolate chip before."

Emily smirked as a woman snatched up the last plate of lemon bars, much to the chagrin of her neighbor next in line.

"Should I tell them that Elsie's famous lemon bars come out of a box?"

"Don't you dare." Helena giggled. "I didn't bring my riot gear."

The sun tucked behind a pile of mottled clouds, and the tourists scattered, making for the nearest sweatshirt shop.

"Whew." Helena flopped into a chair. "I feel like an ear of corn picked over by locusts."

Emily munched at a cookie.

"Careful," she said. "You're starting to sound like a local."

"Why not?" Helena sighed. "This is my home now. Florida is just a sunny memory."

"You can always go back, you know," Emily offered. "You're what, eighteen?"

"Seventeen."

"You could go back for college, if nothing else."

"I don't know if I'd want to." Helena picked blankly at a callous on her palm. "My dad kind of ruined it for me. I have so many fond memories of him tied up in that place. My whole childhood, really. You know, picnics at the beach, that sort of thing." She squirmed through a moment of silence. "I guess it's childish, but now . . . I just don't want to ruin good memories with bad ones. He's just not the man I always thought he was."

"I'm sorry," Emily murmured. *Don't do it. Don't pry.* "Would you mind if I asked what happened?"

Helena hesitated. Emily recognized the awkward dance of tension in her eyes, the play of doubt across her features as she tried to calculate Emily's trustworthiness.

"My dad started cheating on my mom several years ago. One-night stands, sometimes longer flings. She always suspected that something was going on. I think, in a way, she always knew. She just didn't want to believe it." She smoothed a lock of hair between her fingers, tugging at it absently. "The last straw came when he was caught picking up what he thought was a prostitute."

She glanced at Emily, who murmured her horror into a covering hand.

"She was an undercover policewoman, trying to bust johns." Helena blushed painfully. "Soon everyone at school knew, and all of my mother's friends. We just had to get out of there."

Emily opened then shut her mouth. All she had to offer the girl were platitudes: cheap, greeting-card sentiments Helena had surely heard before.

"The worst part is I feel like I've lost my father. Like I don't even know who he is. Like I never knew." Helena's voice grew thick. "Everything I loved about him, all the good things don't matter anymore. I don't know if I can ever forgive him. Just the thought of him makes me sick. I'd like to tell him how he hurt us, but I don't think I could talk to him. Maybe I could email."

Emily thought of Jericho's emails, too often unnaturally blunt. They were better than nothing, she supposed.

"Fathers can be hard to understand," she said, berating herself for the lame advice. "Even the nice ones."

Some comforter she was, she thought as she gnawed at her lip, but what could she say? She realized with a pang that she didn't know enough about fathers to be much help. The two of them sat for a moment, commiserating wordlessly.

"Hey, Em." A voice pierced their thoughts. "How's the bake sale? And who's your lovely assistant?"

Emily smiled at the sight of Grant Mason coming towards them, looking fresh from the river. Helena stiffened at her side.

"Grant, have you been kayaking in the canyon again? You know Bug hates it when you do that."

He smiled sheepishly.

"Mom worries too much. I've been doing this since I was twelve."

"I won't mention it to her." Emily smiled and narrowed her eyes. "Just to spare her the concern."

She felt Helena vibrating beside her.

"Grant, let me introduce you to Helena Jantzen. She just moved here from Florida, and she's been volunteering at the library."

Grant offered his hand. "You're a brave woman, Helena. These bake sales can, well, let's just say they have an enthusiastic response."

Helena smiled—the effect not lost on Grant, Emily noticed —and took his hand.

"Now you tell me." She laughed. "I've got blisters from counting money."

Grant turned her hand over and shook his head solemnly. "Yes, sir, this is the worst case of nickel thumb I've ever seen. I recommend wearing oven mitts to bed tonight."

Helena giggled, and Grant studied her face.

"You look so familiar."

"We're in the same math class," she said. "Mr. Tyler's pre-calculus."

He snapped his fingers, flinging river water onto an angel food cake. "That's it." He smiled at Emily. "The lady is smart, too."

Someone hollered from the street. Grant shot a wave to a group of dripping youths.

"I've gotta go." He grinned. "The river waits."

"Be careful!" Emily called after him.

She hated to admit it, but she worried about him too. Watching Ian and Rebecca's boy grow up was like having a son of her own. He even gave her a card every Mother's Day.

"He is so cute." Helena smiled, watching Grant's broad shoulders disappear from sight.

"He's a good guy," Emily said. "Really genuine."

One of a dying breed, she wanted to add, but didn't. They fell back into a comfortable silence, each lost in her own thoughts. Without meaning to, Emily began to brood. Why couldn't people stay together? Why did once-happy marriages inevitably end in divorce? Even Murray, a supposedly unmolested slice of Americana, replete with small-town charm and values, was in truth populated by single mothers, widowers, pregnant teenagers, and men hiding from their alimony payments. Even in Murray, few marriages held strong. She thought of Ian and Bug, still bliss-fully wed after twenty years. She had asked them once what their secret was, hoping for some practical advice. Bug had launched into an explanation of their religious beliefs, some-thing Emily immediately tuned out. She didn't ask again.

It wasn't that she held anything specific against organized religion. Her own experiences in church as a child, while bor-ing, held nothing to scar her. Religion just wasn't practical. It really didn't offer her anything she didn't already have or couldn't get for herself. She supposed there might be a God somewhere. If she ever needed him, she'd look him up.

"Who are these folks?" Helena's whisper interrupted her thoughts.

"Will and Selma Sutton," Emily said, eyeing the couple as they approached. They too were still happily married, after ten years and two kids. How did they do it? She remembered with an inward sigh that they went to Ian's church. Maybe faith was the key. Or maybe they thought divorce was grounds for eternal punishment.

"Hi, Will, Selma. What are you guys up to on this gor-geous Saturday?"

"Well, Ms. Blyton," Will always spoke with a twinkle in his eye, "we're just strolling the river walk, debating the merits of four-square over dodge ball."

Selma gave him a playful shove. "I say dodge ball is too violent for gym class."

"And I say that the kids don't burn off enough energy playing four-square." He ruffled his wife's blond bob.

Emily turned to Helena. "If you haven't already guessed by their stimulating conversation, Will and Selma are both teachers at Murray Elementary. Will teaches P.E., and Selma is our resident social studies expert. Will's also the head of our volunteer firefighter unit. And this is Helena."

Helena nodded, obviously amused by the disparity in their sizes as they engaged in mock battle. Selma was well over a foot shorter than Will, but feisty.

"Listen, bub, until we get a real school nurse and I can stop playing Florence Nightingale between classes, dodge ball is just too much. I had to stop in the middle of my Magna Carta lesson last week to tend to Vincent's head wound."

"Head wound?" Will howled. "It was a scratch and probably self-inflicted. You know how those third-graders are. Vincent's always got his finger in his face, usually up his nose."

"Helena," Selma said, laughing as Will led her away, "we're so glad you're here. This town could use some fresh blood. You'll have to come to our end-of-summer bash next month."

"The Suttons are famous for their parties," Emily explained. "There's the end-of-summer bash on Labor Day, a Christmas party in December—oh, don't miss that one." She clutched her chest. "Selma's eggnog is to die for. There's also a variety of spring and summer barbecues. The whole town's invited. They're really a lot of fun."

Helena nodded.

"Well." Emily looked at the barren tables before them. "I think this bake sale is officially over."

Elsie appeared to count the cash box while Emily and Helena folded the tables.

"My, this is more than I expected. We'll be able to buy those updated encyclopedias. Maybe some computers. Thank you for all your help, girls." She beamed at them. "We couldn't have done it without you."

Emily smiled at her use of the royal "we." Yes, sir, Elsie

was prime manager material. She kissed the older woman soundly on the cheek.

"It's always a pleasure, Elsie."

She turned to Helena.

"Would you like me to walk you home?"

She cursed her maternal instincts and her curiosity for getting the best of her as she realized how stupid that sounded.

"That's OK." Helena smiled and waved toward Main Street. "I live just up the road."

"So does everyone in this town." Emily chuckled. "Welcome to Murray."

As Helena wandered up the street, her solitary figure fading with the afternoon, Emily felt herself flatten under a familiar cloud. She was alone again. Self-pity settled into a knot beneath her ribs. Maybe she needed another hobby, she thought as she dragged herself home. Maybe she needed another job or another pet.

"Maybe I just need to grow up," she mumbled.

Staying active, she knew from long years of experience, was the key. She would write to Jericho when she got home and catch her up on the doings of Murray. The tidbits of small-town gossip that Emily often sent seemed to gain the most response from her daughter, although her last message had spurred no reply at all. Emily sighed as she trudged through the trees. She didn't want to be a pest, of course, but she was the girl's mother.

Thinking of mothers, she wondered where Helena's was. Unpacking the house, she supposed, and nursing her wounds. Jericho was the only thing that had gotten Emily out of the house after Rick left, and even that was a struggle. Maybe she should stop by, but what would she say? *Don't worry, you'll survive? Suck it up or join a convent? Men are pigs?*

A mournful cry stilled the woods, soon answered by another keening howl. Though wolves weren't common in Murray, several had settled in the woods around Emily's cabin, drawn, no doubt, by the fat rabbits and lack of people. Moscow would be restless at home, trotting laps around the living room and whining to join the pack.

"I know how you feel, boy." She caved in a rotten log with the heel of her boot as she tromped heavily home. "I know how you feel."

FOUR

LIGHTNING flickered above the skylight in Emily's loft. She twitched from a restless sleep, rolled her face beneath a pillow, and growled along with the thunder. Another Sunday morning and, glory be, it was storming. If only it would rain.

After an unseasonably dry winter and month after summer month of parched skies, the town, along with most of the state, was in a drought. At first, Murray had reveled in the extra attention as city dwellers from the eastern half of the state flocked to the mountains to escape the oppressive heat of their asphalt suburbs and downtown lofts, but soon the tiny oasis had wilted with the rest of the west in the glare of an unrelenting sun. The aspens yellowed early, leaves seizing as they separated from their branches with arthritic pops, while the pine trees rid themselves of needles with a collective shake. The herds of resident elk that normally brought tourists flocking stuck to the relative cool of the high country, preferring not to roast themselves into jerky along Main Street. Even the old-timers had to dredge deep into their memories to recall such a dry spell. And every afternoon the clouds gathered over Murray, sparking with lightning, but no rain. Mother Nature was such a tease.

Emily tied on a robe and said a silent prayer to the precipitation gods as she slipped downstairs. Her stomach rumbled at the thought of waffles, but they were too much work for just one person. Cereal would have to suffice.

"One bitter divorcée's special, coming up," she muttered as the flakes pinged into the bowl.

The day loomed ahead of her, gray and empty, as she crunched through breakfast on the couch. She could finish soldering the window, she supposed, but she was already ahead of schedule, and a day cooped up in the garage wasn't appealing. Moscow snoozed at her feet, snout buried in his paws. He needed a walk, of course, but that would only take so long. She thought of the scrapbook supplies Elsie had given her last Christmas, now buried in the hall closet, and grimaced around the raisin bran. A good project for a rainy day, but pasting together bright construction-paper snippets of her past with glitter and smiles wasn't exactly her style. She tossed the bowl into the sink with a sigh. She could always go back to bed, pretend she was sick, let Moscow snuggle at her feet as she reread a dog-eared romance. It was pathetic, she knew, but strangely appealing.

Elsie's face hovered in her mind as she dragged up the stairs. What was it Elsie wanted?

The research for the museum. Emily yawned, her brain sparking like an old bulb. Town Hall would be open. Like most government operations in small tourist towns, it rarely closed, and she could easily find the information she needed in the public records department. Researching her genealogy would be interesting, a good way to kill a few hours, if nothing else. She hung her robe back on its hook and slipped into the shower.

Maybe this was the hobby she'd been looking for.

A welcome spattering of rain cut Moscow's walk short, and Emily arrived in town by eleven o'clock, eager to get on with the day. The sidewalks were clotted with sightseers snapping pictures, asking for directions, and complaining about the lack of elk, while the town's true residents took to the hills, hiking, biking, sleeping off hangovers from the night before, and skittering off to church. Murray was a day-tripper's town on Sunday mornings, full of strange faces and the awkward jostling of the lost. Emily murmured apologies as she slipped through a crowd of glaring teenagers on the steps of Town Hall and into the lobby.

"Well 'ello there, Miz Bly'in. Wha' brings you to our luv-ly seat of government on dis fine day?"

"Hi, Horace." She smiled at the slightly oafish, middle-aged man behind the information desk. "I'm here to check out some public records stuff for Elsie. How's your cat doing?"

"Tanks for askin', luv." He adjusted his goggle-ish glasses. "Me kitty's doin' fine—'ad a bit uv a scare last week wit' a 'air-ball, though."

Emily knew better than to ask, but couldn't help herself. "What's with the accent, Horace?"

"Oh, I'm glad you noticed," he beamed. "The community theater is holding open auditions for *My Fair Lady* next month. I've go' to be a perfect British gent by then, I do."

Emily bit the inside of her cheek and smiled encouragingly. "That's wonderful. I'm sure you'll get a great part."

"Public records, you said?" He tipped an imaginary bowler and motioned toward the basement. "That way."

Emily thanked him and bustled down the stairs into the whitewashed fluorescence of the basement, hiding a grin behind her hand.

"Hello?"

Her voice barely sounded in the cavern of a room that somehow managed, in the midst of the drought, to smell damp. She would never understand herself, moping one moment because she was lonely and sighing with relief to be left alone the next.

She moved between the rows of filing cabinets, scanning the plaques that listed their contents. Strange coincidence that Elsie should ask her to work on this project. She didn't know much about her family beyond her parents and her one grandfather who had survived into her childhood, and even he was glowering and dim. Come to think of it, she didn't know that much about her own parents. They had been unhappily married for twenty-one years before her mother died, devastating her father while providing her mother with what Emily suspected was a sweet release. Not that her father was so terrible. He was never excessively violent or cruel, the way some of her friends' fathers were, but he was difficult, unpredictable, and draining with a quiet hostility. He grew sullen after her mother died, consumed with his own gnawing criticisms, finally void of the flashes of warmth and rare smiles that had made him tolerable before. She had asked him about her grandparents only once, when he was in the mellow stage of his third drink after dinner. His mumbled reply about their fight with the landlords in Ireland and their immigration to America had discouraged further questions.

Emily sighed, grown suddenly grim at the task before her. How far back did Elsie want her to go? Her great-grandfather? Her great-great-grandfather? Blyton wasn't that common of a name, but still it was a lot of digging to do, considering she had next to nothing to go on. Might as well start with the present.

The drawer labeled "Birth Certificates" shimmied open with a musty breath. She filed through the "*B*s," found John Blyton halfway through, and paused. How strange to hold that yellowed parchment in her hands, to look at her father's tiny footprints inked beside his name. He had been a child once too.

"How did he forget so fast?" she whispered. She filed the paper back into place and turned to the next document as she tried to keep the memory of her father from crowding her in the narrow aisle.

"Daniel Brothers?" Emily frowned. "Where's mine?"

She flipped through the papers with mild irritation.

"It should be right here, with Dad's."

She started from the beginning and searched the drawer, thumbing page by page in case the papers were stuck together. What had happened to her birth certificate? Surely, the town had a record of her somewhere. Out of sheer curiosity, she pulled open a neighboring drawer and thumbed through the marriage certificates.

"Emily Blyton and Richard Hadden," she read, surprised that their divorce papers weren't stapled to the back.

There it was, the only proof that she existed, she thought wryly. Just what Elsie wanted: the history of her failed marriage.

She dragged a chair over to a drawer of unorganized periodicals and scrounged gently through the stacks of brittle newspapers. Birth announcements in the *Murray Daily News* were expected of new parents back then, almost required. Surely, there would be some mention of her there. She found the weekend edition from the week she was born and slid the paper carefully from the pile. Grocery circulars fluttered to the floor, advertising ridiculously cheap cuts of meat and poultry. Thunder rolled outside as she leafed through the pages. The "Births and Deaths" column held no trace of her, though half a dozen other parents celebrated the joy of a new child.

"Geez, didn't they even care that I was born?"

She closed the paper and slid it back into the stack, catching the tiny blurb on another paper as she turned away:

"Local couple welcomes new baby."

She eased the paper out, checked the date and followed the blurb to the appropriate page.

"Locals John and Amy Blyton had reason to celebrate this week," she read, "as they learned that the adoption papers they submitted to the state of New York were successfully received and accepted."

Adoption papers.

The whole world seemed to stutter and hesitate around Emily for a moment as the words sank in. She swallowed and turned the page.

"Baby Emily, named after Amy's grandmother, was joyfully received into the Blyton family earlier this week. Emily will be christened at Good Shepherd Lutheran Church in Denver next week in a service for family and friends."

The paper fluttered to her feet.

"I wasn't adopted."

There was plenty of proof. There were countless pictures of her squalling as an infant in her mother's arms. Stories of her childhood antics, her first word, her first smile. *But no pictures from the hospital. No stories of the night I was born.*

A set of icy spurs rolled down her spine. She was a Blyton. It was all she had ever been.

She scanned the grainy picture of her parents. Had they really ever been that young? They were smiling, heads bent together, her mother clutching a bundled blanket in her arms.

"Baby Emily comes home," the caption read. The checkered blanket, draped to cover the newborn's face, had been Emily's favorite as a child, given to her on the night she was born, her mother always said. It was strange, though. Emily tilted the picture. That looked like water in the background. They were perched on the steps of a building overlooking some kind of bay. There weren't any bodies of water like that in Colorado. Her eyes were drawn to a faint length of lettering along the side of the photograph: "Photo courtesy of the State of New York, Adoptions Division."

"Oh, God," Emily whispered.

A fluorescent bulb began to rattle above her like a wounded thing, and Emily thought she might throw up. What if it was true?

"It can't be." She rubbed the picture absently with her thumb, holding the memory of their faces as a shield against the awful truth, but the evidence was right there. What more proof did she need? Emily felt herself weaving and clutched at the back of the chair.

"Oh, God, who am I?"

❧

"Ian!"

The corrugated tin siding of Ian's workshop hurt Emily's fist. No one had answered at the front door or the garage. Where could they be?

"Ian!" she yelled, hating the desperation in her voice.

When had she ever heard herself sound so frantic? A

memory of Jericho wandering into the woods as a toddler came to mind. They had searched the forest for two panicked hours before they found her holding a tea party beneath the porch.

"Ian!"

There was a metallic rattle and a scraping sound as Ian opened the door. Emily thought she might cry.

"What? What is it?" He grabbed her wrist. "What happened?"

His face and faded jeans were smeared with grease, and his pupils were wide beneath the brim of his battered baseball cap. She suddenly felt ridiculous. Poor Ian. As a pastor he had conducted enough funerals to expect trouble from an ordinary day, and she in her haste had sent his imagination into high gear.

"Is it Grant?" The wrench fell from his hand.

"No! No, everyone's fine. No one died," she explained hastily, feeling more foolish by the moment.

Why had she come running to the Masons' anyway? They were her best friends, her spiritual advisors, she supposed, although she'd never considered herself much of a spiritual person, and she needed to know what was going on. If there was a God, he surely had a hand in this.

"Everything's all right." She wandered around to the front of the house and flopped down on the porch. Ian left the wrench in the driveway and followed. "I just wanted to talk to someone."

"Oh." His lanky frame sagged with relief. "If there's one thing I can do, it's listen. Sorry it took me so long to get to the door. I was underneath the car."

"I can see that." Emily smiled. "So, how was the service this morning?"

What was she trying to do? Make small talk?

"It was great." He turned his cap around backwards until his sandy hair sprouted in tufts from the sides. "We discovered the meaning of life and all the secrets of the universe. You really should have been there."

She smirked. How did such a wise guy end up working for God?

"So, is there anything specific you want to talk about?" He rubbed his palms together nonchalantly. Obviously there was, and he knew it. It wasn't every day she tried to punch a hole in the siding of his workshop.

"Ian, I have no idea who I am," she blurted, digging at the ground with her toe. "Everything I've always believed about myself, my family, isn't true."

Tears seeped in from the corners of her eyes. She blinked them away. It was no time to fall apart.

"I found out—" She cleared her throat. "—that I was adopted."

Emily couldn't help but watch for his reaction. It wasn't often she dropped a bomb like that on anyone.

"Wow." Ian blinked.

Emily waited in silence. Wow? Was that all he had? No words of wisdom? No spiritual tidbits she could keep in her pocket for the next rainy day?

"Are you sure?"

She nodded, feeling strangely removed. It had sounded even crazier when she said it out loud.

"I was working on this project for Elsie, and I found an old newspaper article about the adoption. About my parents bringing me home from New York."

New York. It sounded like another planet.

"Murray had no record of me. No birth certificate. It's like I don't exist."

"OK." Ian rubbed his chin between his thumb and forefinger, smearing grease along his jaw. "Let's not panic. How can you be sure about this? If this is true, someone has to know about it."

"I can't exactly ask my parents," she said, unable to keep a trace of bitterness from her voice. "Who else knew them around here in the early sixties? Most people moved here later."

Ian stopped suddenly and tapped a blackened finger on her knee.

"Harry. Harry would know."

"Harry," she echoed. "Of course. He's been here longer than anyone. He was so close to my parents."

She climbed up from the porch, dusting off her shorts in a daze. Knowing that the truth, the awful, earth-splitting truth, could likely be found sipping tea in a cabin up the road, she was suddenly afraid.

"Ian." A tremor shook her arm. "I'm not sure I want to know. It's so much easier the other way. I don't suppose I could just forget all this? Pretend that nothing's changed?"

Ian shook his head.

"You know you can't. You of all people, Em, would never let this go." He steered her toward the road. "Let us know what Harry has to say."

She stopped halfway down the driveway.

"Aren't you going to tell me that it doesn't matter anyway?" she asked. "That we're all God's children?"

"Do you want me to tell you that?"

"No."

"Em, you know what I believe. The Bible says that anyone can be God's child through faith in His Son—"

"Yeah." She waved him off as she turned. Boy, that guy never quit. "Yeah, I know."

She crunched down the driveway and turned toward town.

⁂

Murray shone beneath a slick of rain, the sidewalks and deserted streets a uniform gray in the unfamiliar sheen of precipitation. Emily ducked beneath the awnings along Main Street as she wove her way toward Harry's cabin. A copse of aspen sheltered the trail that led to his door, shedding the premature colors of fall, and as she climbed Emily heard a childish voice ring out in her memory.

"The streets of heaven are paved with gold!"

She was a child again beneath those creamy, reaching arms, laughing with a playmate as they swam through the piles of leaves.

"Where did you hear that?"

"At church." Her friend laughed and launched into the trees.

"Paved with gold," little Emily whispered, looking past the veil of yellow to the promise of the sky.

⁂

Up in a cabin on the side of a hill overlooking the town, Harry Heppner's leg began to throb. The doctors couldn't explain the very real pain he sometimes felt in a limb that no longer existed, but when the barometer fell or the emotional climate around him changed, his leg began to yell, as real as ever. He held these sparks of light in his ethereal flesh as a talisman against further harm. Surely, he had suffered enough.

45

"What could it be today?" he wondered aloud as he thumped across his living room to peer out at the gray sky.

The tuft of fur at his feet began to grumble.

"What is it, Mutt? What's coming our way?"

He thumped into the kitchen and put the kettle on to boil, forming a silent prayer for any who were suffering nearby. A solitary bead of rain traced down his kitchen window. Not enough moisture to do any good, but a nice change nonetheless. The aspens at the bottom of the hill fluttered as someone passed through them, and Harry strained for a glimpse of the visitor.

"Emily Blyton," he murmured.

She had the look of John Blyton about her. Not his physical appearance, of course, but his mannerisms and the smooth swing of his gait. There were many ways to imprint yourself on a child.

"What brings Emily our way this morning?"

Harry noticed the look on her face and felt his hands begin to tremble.

"I think I know."

Some secrets weren't meant to stay hidden.

⚜

The Heppner cabin rested comfortably beneath the shelter of several massive pines, looking as if it had been there since the beginning of the world or perhaps before. A morsel of fur pranced from one end of the porch to the other, rumbling in the back of its throat.

Emily extended her hand to the tidbit of a dog and let it glean what it could from the scent of her palm.

"Harry?"

The screen door opened with a whine. Harry's wrinkled face beamed from the doorway.

"Emily Blyton." He grinned, hastily tucking his shirt into his pants. "To what do I owe this unexpected delight?"

Emily smiled and took the hand he extended, warm and crumpled with wear.

"Is Mutt out there? If I've told him once, I've told him a thousand times not to bark at visitors."

He hobbled past her into the kitchen, favoring his leg over his perfectly sound prosthesis. She had a feeling he had never grown accustomed to needing its assistance.

"But I suppose it's in his blood to defend his own," Harry cackled. "Can't fight instinct."

A battered kettle puffed on the warm corner of the stove.

"Would you like some tea, dear?"

"I'm fine, but thank—"

"Well, you're going to have some anyway. You look like you're freezing in those shorts. Not," he added with a characteristic twinkle, "that you don't look as pretty as a speckled pup. This is a welcome spell of rain. Not enough to do much good, but nice for a change."

Emily blushed and smiled as she wandered into the hall. She was a grown woman—middle-aged, she thought with distaste—but somehow Harry still managed to make her feel delightfully small. She brushed a fine film of dust from the rows of photographs hung along the wall in neat frames.

"That was my Gloria," he said when she reached a picture at the end, "just a week before we were married. She was so beautiful, I hardly knew what to do with her."

Emily nodded at the smooth brown curls and smiling eyes, still starry beneath the weight of time and glass. She had seen the picture and listened to the story of how Harry and Gloria met several times before, but feigned ignorance when he handed her a steaming mug.

"We met on the sidewalk on a Monday afternoon." He looked into his cup, as though searching the glassy amber for his beloved's face.

"She was coming out of the grocer's with a couple of bags. I was horsing around with my buddies, not a bad group of fellows, but I guess we were a little careless that day. One of them gave me a shove, and before I knew it I was on top of poor Gloria."

He chuckled until tea sloshed over the lip of his mug.

"There were eggs in her hair and on her dress." He laughed again. "She was furious, and I was in love. She was never so pretty as when she was angry. It took me three weeks to convince her to see me again, and by then I knew. She was destined to be my wife. My one great love. Fifty years we were together. Fifty years before the cancer took her."

He handed Emily her tea, grasped her beneath the elbow and steered her into the narrow sitting room, where furniture huddled under afghans and doilies as if Gloria had never left.

"But that's not what you're here to talk about, is it?"

Emily squirmed and tapped at her mug. How exactly was she supposed to do this? She cleared her throat and settled into a chair.

"Well, Harry, you know the most about this town. You've been here longer than anyone else."

Why was it such a difficult question to ask?

"And I know you knew my family pretty well. What I mean is," she glanced up to find him watching her through narrowed eyes, "am I . . . well, this is silly, but . . . was I . . . adopted?"

There, the question was out. Harry would laugh and

thump her on the back. *How absurd,* he would chortle, *what a notion.*

"Yes," he said. Not a moment's hesitation. "Yes, Emily, you were adopted."

"What?"

She teetered at the edge of the chair. He wriggled the mug from her grasp and set it on the table.

"Are you sure?"

"Yes, I'm sure. I was there the night your parents brought you home. I met them in Colorado Springs and drove them back here while they cooed over you, a little pink bundle, in the back seat."

"Why didn't they tell me?" she asked. "Who else knew?"

"Everyone knew," he shrugged. "But Murray was full of retired miners back then, Em. By the time you would have been old enough to understand, most of them had passed on. Your parents didn't tell you because they didn't want you to feel out of place." He huffed defensively. "They loved you like their own, Emily, durned if they weren't going to raise you as a Blyton."

"Why didn't you tell me, Harry? After Dad died, you could have told me."

He studied the twisted roots of his knuckles.

"How was I supposed to tell you something like that? Your father was a good man, if not the most affectionate. I didn't want you thinking less of him." His hands began to tremble. "I'm sorry. I fought with it, wondering if I should tell you, I honestly did, but you were already grieving. I didn't want to make things worse."

She grasped his hands between her own.

"It's OK, Harry." She gave him a watery smile. "You were doing what you thought was best. I appreciate that."

"Durn it all," he groused. "You don't have to be so nice about this. I can only imagine, news like this . . . it's like when those doctors told me they were going to take my leg. It's losing a part of yourself. Maybe something you took for granted all along, but now you wish you could keep. You would give anything to keep it." He winced. "I don't know if I would have fought for my country had I known I'd end up a cripple, but you don't have a choice about this. You're alive, and you are who you are, and you can't undo that."

"No, I can't. But I don't know how to live with it, either. I've got no identity, Harry. I don't know who I am."

"Maybe that's something you can find, in time," he said, "but for now, you're a strong, smart lady, and you've got a lot to be thankful for, not the least of which is a town of friends and people who love you."

Desperation shadowed his eyes. He was only trying to help.

"You're right." She dropped a kiss on his forehead and walked to the door with a measure of self-control that amazed even herself. "Don't worry about me, I'll be fine. It's just a surprise, that's all." Mutt yapped as she reached for the screen door. "Thanks for your honesty, Harry, I really appreciate it."

His grunt was worried as he limped onto the porch.

"It's OK." He patted her shoulder awkwardly. "You'll see."

"I know." She forced a smile and let the door swing shut behind her.

Emily stumbled down the hill in a fog, finally understanding why Harry constantly reached for the leg that wasn't there. How could she scratch an itch she couldn't find? How could she mourn the loss of the person she had thought she was, the person who'd never existed to begin with? Branches

50

snapped beneath her boots as she groped for footholds on the graveled path.

Where am I going?

It was a rhetorical question, asked from a distance in a voice she hardly recognized, but she already knew the answer. It didn't matter where she went. Her home, her friends, her memories were suddenly the ornaments of a stranger's life.

I don't belong anywhere.

She struggled through the woods, mindless of the hour or the barbed branches nipping at her calves. Habit led her up a steep embankment to a broad boulder high above the town. It was where she always ended up in times of trouble, in the silence of the mountain, the sanctuary of the forest and the still press of the thin air. It was where she had come when her mother died, clipped suddenly from a winding mountain road by another car; where she'd faced her fears when she discovered that she was pregnant; where she'd mulled over Rick's proposal with the bittersweet inkling that she was leaving her youth behind forever.

She grasped a trunk as she climbed onto a rock worn deep by water and years, and settled into her favorite crevice. The canyon wound away to her left, the river flashing briefly through a gap in the woods. To her right, innumerable trees marched over the hills into eternity, brooding firs and groves of aspen glowing in wayward shafts of sun. Murray's roads and rooftops crouched between the hills in the valley directly below her, huddled beneath the overhang of the mountains as if on borrowed time. She watched a car trace the winding path through town toward the freedom of the highway and wondered what life had been like for the engineers who had molded the town around those hulks of changeless granite so long ago, forcing civilization into the wilderness like a bone broken to fit the cast. Looking back, it was painfully obvious that, like the town, she had never really belonged.

Memories crowded in on her as she clung to the rock, and familiar voices slipped through to her on a breeze.

❧

"She's quite the little artist, you know."

It was her mother, talking to one of the many faceless relatives Emily could never keep straight.

"I wonder where that came from," he had murmured, eyeing Emily as if she weren't real, as if she weren't standing *right there.* Her mother flushed, a look of irritation and embarrassment on her face as she reached for Emily, hesitated, and drew back her hand.

"There's plenty of artistic talent on John's side of the family."

An older Emily watched intently as her father turned a rough block of wood on the lathe in their garage. She knew, with the confidence only a proud twelve-year-old possesses, that in her father's hands the splintered lump would soon become a shiny table leg, the most elegant table leg ever to grace their kitchen. Golden tendrils curled to the floor beneath his touch.

"Can I try?" she whispered reverently, surprised by her audacity.

Dad's workshop was much like a museum: a place to listen and learn, to be seen but not heard. To her amazement, he handed her the chisel and circled his arm around her, guiding her hand over the wood.

"That's it," he murmured. "You're doing fine."

She beamed. He chuckled, a priceless sound because it was so rare.

"I think you have your grandfather's hands," he said as she settled back into his arms.

❧

How absurd! Emily banged her heels against the boulder and chucked a rock at the distant rooftops below. She didn't have her grandfather's hands. She didn't even know who her grandfather was.

And neither did her father! The liar!

"How could they have lied to me for so long?" she whispered to the trees.

All of the stories, the hours spent poring over photo albums in her mother's lap, the family tree her father helped her map for a school project when she was fourteen, the constant comments that she had her mother's eyes, her father's mouth —they were all lies.

She ran her hands through her hair, the thick locks of sandy gold finally making sense. There hadn't been a blond in the Blyton clan for as long as anyone could remember. No wonder she'd spent so much of her childhood fighting the feeling that she was just a novelty.

"I'm not even Irish, am I?" she wondered aloud. "I don't know what my family's medical history is. What if my real mother had cancer? What if I'm genetically prone to diabetes or Alzheimer's?"

The implications were staggering. And what about Jericho? What would Jericho do if she knew?

"I can't even tell my daughter where she came from."

Emily huddled against the rock as this new fear pulled the warmth from her bones. Jericho would find a way to blame her somehow. Would she sever the tie between them completely?

Cut off all contact? Emily could hear their voices screaming in her mind already.

I can't lose my daughter. Tears threatened her eyes.

But what could she do? Bury the truth? Perpetuate the lie through another generation? Secrets like this had a tendency to unearth themselves at the worst moments, and Emily had never had the heart for much deception.

"I've got to find the truth. I've got to have something to tell her."

But where would she look? What would she find? Emily was suddenly weary. She climbed unsteadily to her feet, brushing gravel from her legs.

Tomorrow. Tomorrow she would start her search. Somewhere in Murray there had to be some evidence of who she really was. Jericho's eyes flashed before her, glassy with tears.

"I don't care if I have to dissect this town brick by brick," Emily breathed. "I'm going to find it."

The mingled scents of the forest settled over her at the head of the trail, a mournful benediction as she passed beneath a twisted fir. She stopped and turned back toward the tree. She had helped her father bury her mother near such a tree in the old Murray cemetery, her adolescent hands shaking as she obediently laid a flower on the fresh soil. She had pressed her face against the curling bark of the trunk as her father said his last goodbye, a broken man for the first and last time in her memory. For weeks after, the memory of the pungent sap had hung over her like a burial shroud, an incense mingling with one tragic thought: *I have only my father now.* She had wondered how they would get along without Mom, the faithful liaison between them.

"Do you want to talk about this?" he had grunted that night over the chicken she'd somehow managed to prepare.

She had glanced at his work-roughened hands and blinked away a stream of tears. What was there to say? Her mother was dead. She was sad. She was afraid. What she wouldn't have given to crawl into his lap, to turn her face into his chest and cry. *What a ridiculous thought.*

"No," she had whispered.

Now, Emily leaned into the fir and blotted her eyes on a sleeve, letting the memory seep away.

"I have no father." She felt truly alone for the first time in her life. "I never did."

FIVE

GUESS, Mommy, guess!" The childish voice, happy and carefree, echoed in Emily's dreams. She twitched beneath a mound of blankets as her subconscious reeled out the past in vivid colors.

Jericho hopped around the fabric store with great delight, trailing a length of checkered cloth behind her. She was surprisingly persistent, even for a seven-year-old.

"Who am I?" she demanded, wrapping the fabric around her head in a lopsided turban. Emily set down the package of buttons she had been scrutinizing and looked her daughter over.

"Lawrence of Arabia?" she guessed. Jericho screwed her face into a scowl beneath the drooping headdress.

"Who?" she asked.

"Ummm. Never mind." Emily held up a yard of lace. She had to find the finishing touch for Jericho's new dress. "How about Snoopy?"

"*Snoopy?*" Jericho gagged on the word.

Funny, Emily thought, six months ago Snoopy was all her daughter could talk about. Scrawled sketches of the chubby pooch still hung from her walls. How quickly she changed.

"You're not trying," Jericho accused. "Who am I?"

Emily sighed. "I have no idea," she confessed. "Are you an animal, vegetable, or mineral?"

Jericho rolled her eyes. *Don't you know anything?* they seemed to say.

It's too early for this, Emily thought. *I still have several years before the perpetual grimace of adolescence sets in.*

"I'm Daddy," Jericho moaned, exasperation oozing from every pore.

Emily raised her eyebrows wearily.

"You're Daddy?" she asked. "What do you mean, sweetie?"

"Well . . ." Jericho began in a voice that implied that spending one weekend a month with her father made her an expert on the man. "Daddy tied a shirt over his head, like this," she bunched the fabric into a makeshift knot, "when we were fixing the car."

"Ohhh, of course," Emily murmured, hiding her distaste in a spool of colored ribbon. Fixing the car? That's how Rick spent quality time with his daughter? He could at least have taken her to the zoo. She consoled herself with the thought that it was only one weekend a month. It was all she had offered of Jericho, and he hadn't asked for more. At least they were spending some time together, her daughter and . . . her daughter's father, regardless of what they were doing.

Aware that Jericho was suddenly and strangely quiet, Emily turned to find her poking somberly at a ball of yarn. Emily pulled out a chair and sat down beside her.

"What's wrong, honey?" she asked. "We're almost done shopping."

Jericho dipped her head and mumbled something into the ball. A tear dripped onto the yarn.

"What was that?" Emily asked, smoothing Jericho's hair back from her face.

"I miss Daddy," she whispered, tugging at the yarn. Emily went cold. Was her daughter saying that she preferred her father? Fixing cars and lukewarm Spaghetti-O's to the love and comfort of home? She swallowed before she trusted herself to speak.

"Would you like to spend more time with him, Jericho?" She couldn't bring herself to ask Jericho if she wanted to live with him in Denver instead of out in the backwoods with her.

Jericho shook her head. Emily thought she would melt with relief.

"It's not that fun being with Daddy," Jericho whispered, as if she were confessing a shameful secret. "He watches TV a lot, and I have to sit and watch him and not say anything when we go bowling." She sighed, a grown-up sound incongruous with her petite frame.

"I miss him because . . ." Jericho fished for the right words in the ball of yarn. "I don't know him. And he doesn't know me. He made me wear a pink shirt last time," she scowled. "I hate pink."

"I know, sweetie," Emily sighed. "Your father may not be the best at knowing what you like, but he does love you, and he is trying."

Is he? she wondered. Maybe not, but what else could she tell her daughter, who built her ideas of the world solely on Emily's word?

"Let's get out of here." She smiled. "I'm in the mood for some ice cream."

Jericho brightened at the suggestion and skipped through the checkout line ahead of her. Emily lagged behind, fingers trembling as she wrote the check. How much longer would ice cream cones placate her daughter? How long until the pain of an absent father turned her against her mother as well?

"Wait up, sweetie. I'm coming."

It was all she could do to keep up. It was all she could do.

❦

Emily groaned from beneath her comforter. Moscow snuffled at the end of the bed, burying his snout beneath the covers at her feet. Jericho's voice still rang in her mind: *Who am I, Mommy? Who am I?*

She rolled out of bed and lurched for the dresser. What had she done? She had unwillingly, unknowingly, passed the curse of her own life onto her daughter.

"She doesn't know," she whispered hoarsely to the mirror, straining through the veil of shadows to meet her own eyes. "She doesn't know her father any more than I know mine."

Emily shivered in the cold breath of dawn. What had she done to drive Rick away? How had she managed to deprive both herself and her daughter of their fathers?

"Oh, God," she moaned, wrapping her arms around her thin frame, "what have I done?"

What have I done? Why did you do this to me is more like it.

Ian believed in a God of love.

"No." She whispered in the cold blue room. "There is no God. Not one who cares."

Was that the legacy she wanted to leave her daughter? A doubtful, fearful, faithless life? She turned away from the mirror, unwilling to watch the hard lines of her face in the mocking rose-colored light. What else was there to give Jericho? The promise of a God who was essentially a no-show? Who wasn't around when you really needed him? That would do her a lot of good. Emily felt something slamming shut inside herself, the familiar locking of a door.

"Grow up." She reached for her robe. "Life is what we make of it, nothing more."

Moscow sighed and slid to the floor as if to say he knew another long day was ahead.

SIX

EMILY slipped a fresh shirt over her head, pulled a comb through her wet hair, and sat down in front of the fireplace to lace her running shoes. Moscow cracked one eye from the couch, spied Emily's shoes, and let out a mournful yowl.

"Oh, all right," she muttered. "I guess you can come."

He slid to his feet and shook his fur before trotting over to lick her face. Emily plucked a dust bunny from his whiskers and ran her hands over his back with a sigh. Working had been the only way to get her mind off of everything after she'd crawled out of bed at four o'clock. Moscow had wedged himself beneath her workbench and swept the floor with his shaggy haunches in the process.

"Such a good boy," she crooned, scratching the knot on his head. "How can I say no?"

He was out the front door and down the path toward town before she found her keys.

"C'mon, dog. Don't leave me now." She sighed. "You're all I've got."

She kicked a pinecone along the needle-strewn path and wondered what to do next. After hovering over her computer for an hour, fingers poised like birds of prey above the keys, she'd given up on writing to Jericho. She needed more information, something more to go on before she unloaded this whole mess on her daughter. Besides, email probably wasn't the way to break that kind of news. She could only imagine the nasty reply she'd receive.

Then again, at least it would be a reply.

Another thought struck her. How was she supposed to learn anything about herself or her real family's whereabouts without raising suspicion? Murray was, after all, the quintessential small town, complete with a healthy and active grapevine, and too many questions regarding her parents or her birth would undoubtedly get its juices flowing. She could almost hear Stanley's nasal drone above the heads of tourists: "I was standing right here, folks, when I first heard the news, and I could hardly believe it myself. Emily Blyton was adopted! She'd been living with a lie all her life. There she is now, folks. Let's all wave to the poor lady as she goes by."

Emily threw off the thought with a shiver as Moscow's staccato yap spurred her down the trail. What had he unearthed this time? A nest of squirrels? A wayward rabbit? She prayed it wasn't a skunk.

"Moscow!" she called, startled by her own voice in the silent woods. Was that what she really sounded like? What faceless relative had given her such a thin, small voice?

"C'mere, boy! What is it?"

The bark graveled into a whine, and Emily picked up her pace. She lost her footing and slid past the sharp turn in a cloud of dust, catching a glimpse of them as she skittered past. Their heads were bent together in the fickle shadows of the aspen grove, Harry perched on a fallen log with his cane beside him and Moscow licking his trembling hands between urgent yowls, and she had to admit they made a nice picture as she flew by. Emily killed her inertia in the crook of a tree and hiked her way back to them, seeing as if for the first time how frail Harry was. She had never seen him so drawn, a transparent shadow shifting with the trees.

"Harry!" She fell to her knees, moving Moscow aside with a gentle shove. "What are you doing out here? You shouldn't be tromping through the woods by yourself."

He smiled and shook his head, catching at a ragged breath. A flush of color crept back into his face, and Emily loosened her grip on his knee.

"Well, you're just the person I was coming to see," he puffed. "I remembered something, late last night as I was hauling myself to bed, that I thought you might want to know. That's the trouble with old age." He gripped her bicep with a gnarled hand. "Your memory works a little slower than it should."

Emily smiled at the tender throb of her heart. If only she could choose her family, Harry would be the first she picked.

"I would have come to you," she protested, failing to sound stern. "The hike to my place is too much for you."

Harry nodded and lifted watery eyes to the trees.

"I guess at some point we get old, don't we?" he asked softly, beneath the moan of the rubbing branches. He sighed and rubbed one hand over the other. "It's funny. Somewhere in my mind I still think I'm a young man. I was such a brazen cuss. Stupid, actually." He grinned. "But I thought I owned the world. These woods were my playground, but now," he waved

65

a hand toward the sky, "now my knees creak loud enough to scare away the critters."

Emily rose from her knees, suddenly conscious of the cracking in her own joints, and took a seat beside him. Moscow flopped into a bed of nearby moss and began to roll.

"It happens to the best of us," she said. "It's inevitable. We grow old and . . ." She realized too late that there was no pleasant way to end that sentence and chided herself for her insensitivity.

"I'm glad I won't be around to see it happen to you." Harry smiled, a pinched look that signaled the stiffening of his joints. "In my mind, you'll always be young and strong, just like you are today."

Emily wanted to laugh at that, but supposed forty-one looked like the prime of life to eighty-five.

"C'mon." She looped her arm beneath his elbow and helped him to his feet. "Let's walk back to town, and you can tell me why you were willing to risk life and limb in the wilderness to find me."

His eyebrows bristled like caterpillars.

"Why, to be seen on the arm of the prettiest gal in Murray," he cackled. "We'll have the whole town talking if we're not careful."

Emily laughed, a rueful sigh of a sound, and led him down the hill toward town.

⊰❈⊱

Emily glanced at Harry from the corner of her eye. They had been walking in silence for half an hour. Moscow barreled on ahead, snapping at chipmunks and clouds. Murray proper lay before them in a network of quaint cobblestone streets and flowerbeds crackling with dry pansies and columbines. What was it Harry wanted to tell her? There was no rushing him, she knew, but was it possible he had forgotten why he came looking for her in the first place? He changed their course abruptly, leading her toward a bench at the edge of town and clearing his throat with monumental importance.

"Let's talk for a while," he said gruffly, motioning for her to take a seat.

Emily's stomach seized suddenly as she wrestled with a vision of Charlton Heston stepping from the wilderness with tablets in his hand. Was it bad news?

"It's been troubling me since yesterday. At first I thought it best not to say anything. You know, let sleeping dogs lie and all. People today overestimate the importance of knowing things. Some things aren't explained for a reason." He patted his palms cautiously against his knees. "Anyway, you seemed so bothered that I hadn't told you about your parents. I figure you can do what you want with what I'm going to tell you." He paused, and Emily sucked at her tongue, trying for some semblance of patience. "In hindsight it's really not important, dear . . ."

"Tell me, Harry."

"I have some information—just a little, mind you—about your family. You know, who your biological folks were."

It was the answer to a prayer she hadn't uttered. Emily was thankful for the bench beneath her.

"That's . . . that's good. I mean, I've been curious. Especially for Jericho. I'd like to be able to tell her where she really comes from."

Harry inched away from her with a look of dismay.

"Jericho loved her grandpa. Your father was wonderful to her. You wouldn't take that away from her?"

"No." She shook her head. "We both loved him. I'm not trying to take away from that. But—" She stopped, horrified at the tears crowding her throat. What was wrong with her? "He wasn't my father, Harry. I have no father now. I have no identity. I need to find both."

Harry nodded.

"Well, I guess I hadn't thought of it that way. I guess you need to know who you are, by blood at least. Everyone else already knows who you are."

"That's because I've always made it on my own, Harry. I've had to. I've always gone it alone because no one else was there to help, but honestly, I've never felt like I belonged." Her voice fell to a whisper. "Not to anyone or anything. I never felt really . . ." she grappled with the word, "*loved* . . . by anyone. Not even Dad. He always knew I wasn't his. I'm no one's. I'm nobody." She shrugged. "I don't know why it's important for me to know the truth, but it is."

He eyed her in silence for a long moment.

"Your father told me once, after one too many beers, that he knew you'd grow up to be a fine young lady because your mother—your birth mother, that is—came from such a fine family. He was jabbering by that time, a lot of nonsense, but I did catch a few things. Her maiden name was Tilberg. Her family was from Manhattan. Her father made his fortune selling steel."

He spoke each fact as a separate and distinct thought, memorized and mulled over countless times.

"Manhattan?" Emily echoed dumbly. It was a world away. "My family was wealthy? Why did she give me up?"

Then she snorted derisively at her own question. She wasn't that naïve. "Of course. Illegitimate children aren't exactly popular in high society, huh?"

Harry fidgeted beside her. "Now, Emily, don't you go talking like that. This is why I didn't want to tell you. It stirs up nothing but trouble."

She laid a hand on his arm. "I'm not upset," she said. "I'm glad you told me. I'm sure this information will be very helpful." She paused for a moment. Would he worry? "I'm going to try to find them, you know."

He nodded. "I figured you would. It's not in your blood to let things be. So, what happens next? Off to New York?"

Emily pinched her forehead as she thought. "I need to tie up a few loose ends first, but yeah, I guess I'm going to New York. I guess that would be the logical place to start."

Bug would take Moscow for her. She needed to see how many orders she had waiting at Song's.

"Emily?"

"Mmm? I'm sorry, did you say something?"

"I said, I imagine Jericho will be pleased to see you."

Emily raised an eyebrow. Since the first mention of New York, the question had been picking at her. Would Jericho be happy to see her? Should she even tell her daughter she was coming?

In a flash, the memory surfaced. Moscow whining beneath the table, Jericho sobbing in her room, Emily fighting for a shred of self-control. *Deep breaths,* a voice warned her, *she's only fifteen.* After a shaky ten-count, Emily climbed the stairs to Jericho's room. They would talk like civilized people. She knocked softly.

"Honey, we need to talk about this. May I come in?"

The door flung open with such force Emily heard the hinges groan. Jericho stood trembling before her, panting with the wrath of a wounded animal. The heavy tracks of makeup, so carefully smudged around her eyes that morning, streamed down her cheeks in a ghoulish reversal of the face nature had given her. The chains wrapped artfully around her throat in a statement of what Emily could only guess was defiance glittered and bobbed as she spoke.

"Oh, yes, dear Mother," she crooned, "by all means, come in for a chat. I really only have one thing to say to you, though."

Emily braced herself.

"Leave . . . me . . . alone!" Jericho screamed and heaved the door shut with a muffled, "I hate you!"

Emily hid in the garage, crying in silence until evening fell.

Now, willing away the memory of Jericho's words, Emily blinked and shook her head. Harry was staring at her, wondering why she hadn't responded.

"Of course," she said brightly. "I'm sure I'll have some quality time with Jericho while I'm there."

The lie sounded so natural, she almost believed it. And why not? Emily squirmed with sudden frustration. Why shouldn't she have the kind of relationship with Jericho that other mothers had with their daughters? She dreamed about it daily: laughing with Jericho over popcorn and old movies on the couch, struggling under the happy weight of shopping bags as they stopped at a café for lunch, marching through piles of glittering snow in search of the perfect Christmas tree, bemoaning the single life together and sharing tidbits of dating advice. She bit her lip as reality crept like a fog into her heart. Her fantasies were wildly improbable. They always would be. Emily cleared her throat. *A few more minutes of this and I'll be blubbering.*

"New York is a long piece away," Harry muttered. "Quite far."

He was obviously hedging an issue, but what?

"Have you thought about the trip?" he continued. "I mean, how you might get there?"

Emily's heart rolled wildly as she finally understood, and she wondered for a moment if she was about to revisit her breakfast.

"I suppose I'll have to fly," she chirped. "So many details I hadn't thought of." Her palms grew slick. "I'm sorry. I'd better get going."

"By all means." He waved expansively. "Go. Travel. Be young."

She helped him to his feet and gave him a squeeze.

"Thank you, Harry," she said, clinging to his cardigan as if it were the last warm thing she would ever touch. "You've been such a help."

"Anything for you, dear. Anything for you."

She eased him onto the sidewalk in a spill of midmorning sun and watched him totter toward the center of town with a tearing envy. If only she were in Harry's place: safe, wise, beloved. If only her days consisted of watching tourists outside the post office, chatting with friends who passed by, and bedding down each night with the memories of a life well spent. Fear and toil would have no place there, fading with the light of the setting sun. If only she, too, could slip past that horizon.

Emily smirked at a sudden vision of her own funeral as she meandered toward Song Tao's New Age shop on the north side of town. Jericho would be there, sobbing with appropriate guilt about the mother she'd never given a chance, and Ian and Grant and Bug. The whole town would probably turn out, now that she thought about it, and possibly her ex. Maybe her real family would materialize, finding their long-lost daughter in a miracle come too late, to huddle over the grave site beating their chests, weeping and crying out, "Why, God, why?"

Emily stumbled into a planter and shook off the morbid fantasy. *No such luck.* Her life stretched ahead of her, a lonely march without reprieve.

Aspens rustled half-heartedly in manicured clumps from the medians on Main Street, while flaming poppies drooped beneath them, petals splayed open in parched defeat. The Murray High School football team barked commands over the crunch of their helmets and the whoops and hollers of the cheerleaders in an open field.

How strange it would be to leave Murray, where warmth pervaded every brick and branch. It was the only home she had ever known. Where would this journey take her, she wondered, and how long would she be gone? Where would she stay? Was New York as cold and alien as everyone said? Faced with the prospect of spending days, possibly weeks, alone in a hostile place, Emily felt weak. How brave of Jericho, she grudgingly admitted, to leave the safety of Murray for the wild blue unknown. Her daughter had always been more adventurous than she. Jericho lunged at life, often bashing her head in the process, while Emily watched from a safe distance, shouting instructions whenever she could. Jericho shied away from responsibility, while Emily was always in control. She had to be. Who else was going to look out for her? Jericho was truly a free spirit.

"She takes after her father in that regard," Emily muttered, crossing the street.

"Emily!" It was Song, mincing her words precisely. "I'm so glad to see you."

She was so lovely, Emily thought as she watched Song wave from the doorway of her shop, her swollen belly swathed in a breezy summer dress. It was beyond Emily why any man would want to leave her.

"Not much longer now, Song." She smiled and gave Song's belly a hesitant pat. Although not overly tall herself, Emily still felt like an ogre next to her petite Asian friend.

"Oof," Song grunted. "I never thought nine months could go so slowly. Two left." She held up two delicate fingers. "It feels like a lifetime."

"Have you thought of any more names?"

Song heaved a grievous sigh and started into the store.

"Traditional Japanese names sound strange in America. Too difficult for a child to explain to everyone he meets." She wrestled herself onto a stool behind the register. "On the other hand, American names seem so bland. I'll probably just end up calling him John or Fred or Peter."

"Well." Emily leaned against the counter. "There has to be a compromise in there somewhere. What if his first name was traditional, but his middle name was American? That way he could go by his middle name if he found the first one too cumbersome."

"Hmm. Not a bad idea." Song tapped a pencil against her chin. "I have to mull that one over." She turned to Emily. "How did you name your daughter?"

"We didn't actually name her until after she was born. Her father insisted that she was a Jane." Emily's eyes rolled reflexively toward the ceiling. "But I wanted something with a little more spark. The night before I went into labor, I had been watching this news special about archeologists finding the ruins of a city in the Middle East. It had once been an empire of sorts, really strong and well protected with these huge, thick walls." Emily shrugged. "It was called Jericho. I guess I thought it would be a good name. I figured my daughter would need a lot of strength for whatever life threw her."

"And is she strong, like her name?"

"Yes," Emily nodded. "She is." *Strong-willed is more like it.* She cast about for a new topic. "Have you heard anything more from Ling?"

Song grimaced at the name of her ex, and Emily was instantly ashamed. "I'm sorry," she said.

"No." Song held up a placid hand. "I have to talk about him eventually. Better get used to it before the little one starts asking questions." She smoothed her dress over her stomach with a practiced hand. "He's living in Texas, of all places. He still doesn't want anything to do with us, but he said he would send money. To cover his *obligations*." She winced as if pressing on a bruise, and Emily felt the wound beneath her own heart. "I could understand it if this was the result of a fling or a one-night stand, you know? But we were married. I was his wife, and he deserted me—carrying his child—for a younger version."

"Boy, does that sound familiar." Helena appeared from the back room with a clipboard perched on her hip. A pencil poked from her coil of heavy hair.

"What a nice surprise." Emily smiled.

"Helena needed a job," Song explained, dabbing at her eyes, "and I needed someone to do inventory. Doesn't that work out well?"

Helena sidled over to the counter and dropped the clipboard with a sigh.

"So what's the deal?" she asked. "Are all men snakes?"

Song laughed and said something in Japanese. Emily shook her head.

"No. Not all men. Look at Ian Mason or Harry. They're

great guys. I think there are some good guys out there, they're just few and far between."

"Very far between," Song muttered.

Helena shrugged and turned back to her work. Song stepped into her office to find Emily's new orders, cradling the weight of her stomach with a slender arm, and Emily was left alone. There they were, she thought, three vastly different women with the same unfortunate problem. She picked a crystal off the counter and pondered its weight against her palm. Maybe that was why her mother had given her away. Maybe her father had insisted she give the baby up, or like Ling had just run away.

"Maybe it doesn't matter," she murmured, turning the glittering rock over with her thumb. A mother could provide all the love and stability a child needed, right? Men were unpredictable . . . inconvenient. Maybe children didn't need fathers after all. She squinted as a shaft of light broke on the crystal's edge and saw her own father through her open bedroom door, sighing in his recliner after a heavy meal. Mother tucked the sheets around Emily's chin and picked up her favorite book. It was the same ritual every night: story, song, sleep, as comforting as the blankets against her cheek. But her father never came. He never joined in the songs or the stories, and when her mom was sick, Emily went without. *He never really cared.*

"Emily? Are you all right?"

"Yeah." Emily set the crystal down heavily. "Of course. What do we have here?" She reached for the rustling carbon copies in Song's hand.

"You've sold a lot of designs from the shop this month, but no custom orders waiting."

"Good." Emily sighed again. She was becoming downright morose. "I'm going to be out of town for a few days. Would you mind putting new orders on hold for a little while?"

Song nodded. "Not a problem. Where are you going? Anywhere exotic?"

"New York. I guess that's exotic enough, in it's own way." Emily said heavily. Why did she dread it so much?

"Oooh!" Helena's eyes widened. "I'm so jealous. Is this an impromptu vacation?"

"Not really. I've got some family back there I need to see."

"But Emily, New York is too far to drive to, especially in your Bronco." Emily could see Song tabulating the tanks of gas in her head. "And you hate to fly."

Fumes burned Emily's throat as she gasped for air. Clouds of burning jet fuel billowed into the cabin. The plane groaned with an unbearable weight, the sound of the wrenching metal drowned out by the horrified screams. The jumbo jet nosed downward, rocketing toward the earth in a ball of flame. Emily clung to her seat back and wept as the chair popped free of the floor one bolt at a time.

"Emily!"

"I'm sorry." She forced herself to breathe, in and out. "I was . . . just thinking about a dream I had." *A nightmare.*

"You're shaking!"

"I've got to go." She gave Song and Helena each a quick squeeze. "I'll see you soon." They waved her out of the shop with cries of good luck and goodbye.

Emily stumbled onto the sidewalk, weaving toward a bench across the street. If only her legs would obey. She collapsed in a trembling heap. An elderly couple meandered by, spotted Emily, and held out their camera beseechingly.

"Say cheese," she muttered, framing them carelessly as she snapped the picture. They thanked her and tottered away. "What am I going to do?" she moaned, leaning her head against the bench. "I can't get on that plane."

A pungent smell spiked the morning air and drove all thoughts of jet fuel from her mind. As she curled into herself with a feigned preoccupation, Emily decided she preferred the burning rubber of her imagination to the smell of Stanley's pipe. He was standing beneath the awning of his shop, taking his usual mid-morning smoke break and smiling as if he owned the world. She slunk from the bench, her legs gaining new strength, and crept away as he blew a white stream over the town. Stanley Warwick was taxing enough on a good day. She couldn't imagine meeting him now.

"Em!"

"Wha-a-t!" she shrieked at the hand on her shoulder. "Grant!" She wheezed out an expletive. "Sorry. You scared me."

Grant stepped back and eyed her keenly, and Emily felt the strange but familiar sensation of watching Bug's eyes in Ian's face.

"What's got you so jumpy?"

"I'm sorry, I was just thinking."

"Spooked about flying to New York, huh?" He tucked his hands in his pockets and grinned sympathetically. "I know it won't be easy for you."

Emily sagged with relief. One less person to explain her miserable life to. Harry must have talked to Ian, and Bug and Grant of course heard it from Ian. It never occurred to her to resent the fact that her life was common knowledge among them. They were all the family she had. She wanted—no, she needed—their input in every facet of her life. Even Grant's lanky frankness, she suspected, hid wisdom beyond his eighteen years. She sank to a brick planter overflowing with flowers and hid her face with a groan. When was the last time she'd allowed herself to need anyone?

Grant plopped down beside her.

"What is it about flying that bothers you so much?"

"I'm not in control," she wailed, and wondered if she was referring to the plane or to her life at the moment. "How do I know there's not a screw missing somewhere that's supposed to hold the wings on? How do I know the pilot's not drunk? Or a complete moron?"

"OK." Grant rested his elbows on his knees. "Let's say you were in control. Let's imagine you're sitting in the cockpit with the controls in your hand. What would happen?"

"I would die in a burning ball of wreckage hurtling toward some poor farmer's field," she said, "because I don't know how to fly."

"OK, so who should be in control of this plane: Emily Blyton, friend to small animals and glassmaker extraordinaire, or Captain Joe United, expert pilot with thousands of hours of flying under his belt? Sorry, Em, but I'm putting my money on Joe. It's a good thing you're not in control. Sit back and enjoy it."

She nodded, running her hands through her hair. His words made perfect sense. Why, then, was her stomach trying to exit through her throat?

"It's like life," Grant continued, and Emily wondered what he could possibly tell her about life. "I can try to run my own life," he tapped his chest, "but I have limited knowledge, flawed judgment, and I can't see the big picture. Or I can let God be in control of my life. God, who has perfect knowledge of every situation, perfect power, love, and so forth."

Emily sighed. He certainly was Ian's son. Heaven forbid they get through a conversation without bringing up God. Friendship demanded she humor him.

"So, Grant, what does *God* want from me in this situation?"

Grant picked a flower and spun it thoughtfully in his hand.

"He wants you to know, Emily, that regardless of what you find or don't find in New York, He's still, and always will be, your Father."

"I have a father," she said quietly, sliding onto the sidewalk. She thought of the cold granite slab, unadorned, in the Murray cemetery. She had never really mourned the distance between them. *Enough of this.* "I just haven't found him yet."

SEVEN

YOU'RE sure about this?"

Emily nodded, glad for once that she wasn't the emotional type. Bug handed her a tiny plastic tub.

"Snacks," she smiled. "For the journey."

Both Ian and Bug had been careful to avoid the word "flight" at all costs during the long drive to the airport. Some of their euphemisms were downright humorous.

"Will you have a chance to see Jericho?"

"I don't know," Emily hedged. "She doesn't exactly know I'm coming. This was all so sudden, and . . . well, you know how things are with us."

Bug nodded, accepting though she didn't understand.

"I think you should see her. It can't hurt."

Emily nodded and rubbed her temple. A scream rose in her memory until she wasn't so sure.

"Get out of my life," Jericho yelled. "You stupid, controlling witch!"

Emily reeled at the force of her daughter's anger, grasping at the cabin for support as Jericho stormed down the driveway, suitcase tumbling awkwardly in the gravel behind her.

"Baby, please," she pleaded. "I'm sorry about what I said earlier. I didn't mean it the way it sounded. I just think you should—"

Emily choked on the advice she was about to share as Jericho turned back at the end of the drive. A lifetime of anger streamed from her dark eyes as she sized up her mother for what seemed the last time, disappointed yet again. *Why was she so angry?* Fear for her daughter swallowed Emily's pain.

"I'm going to New York," Jericho said quietly. "I'm not coming back."

Emily spent the rest of the night on the steps of the porch, nauseated by the tears she couldn't shed. Her daughter, her only child, was gone.

"You'll call if you need us." Ian grasped her arm as he led her through the terminal. It was a statement, not a question, and Emily felt a wash of love as she resurfaced from the past.

"You guys are the best, dearest friends."

"Don't go getting all mushy on me, soldier," Ian grinned. "You'll be back before you know it."

Emily nodded, swallowing against the lump in her throat. "Don't forget," she whispered, "Moscow likes—"

"To be scratched behind the ears," Bug finished. "We know." She squeezed Emily's hand. "Have a safe trip."

Emily turned toward the gaping gullet of the plane, slowed by the knowledge that she was leaving something precious behind. There was no going back. Her feet hit the gangplank with the weight of her uncertainty, and somehow she knew that she was turning yet another corner. Life would never be the same.

⤛✦⤜

The impossibly thin floor growled violently beneath Emily's feet. She clutched at the armrest, no longer concerned with what her seatmate thought. The plane nosed upward, launching her stomach into her throat. She closed her eyes and thought of Bug and Ian. They were praying for her, whatever that was worth. She could almost see them waiting in the terminal, watching her plane take off.

"Do you think she'll find her family?" Bug would ask.

"God only knows." Ian would shake his head. "God only knows."

A voice broke into her thoughts. It was the captain, calm and assured. Everything looked great, he said, and there were clear skies ahead. Emily pried her fingers from the armrest and focused on the seat in front of her, her eyes drawn to the laminated card in its pocket. *Emergency landing . . . oxygen masks . . . flotation device.*

"Miss!" She groped at a passing attendant. "Could I get a drink?"

"Certainly," the woman smiled. "What would you like?"

How could she be so calm?

"Jack and Coke," Emily barked, eyeing her neighbors self-consciously. What must they think of her?

"I don't normally drink," she murmured to no one in particular.

The drink arrived not a moment too soon. She nursed it between white knuckles, sip after numbing sip, and waited for the world to blur.

"How did I get myself into this mess?" she whispered into the cup. The same way, she supposed, her own mother, her real mother, had gotten into hers. *A wealthy socialite,* she mused, grasping for an image to anchor to. Was she tall or short? Slender or stout? Intelligent?

Obviously not smart enough. She snorted, feeling a pleasant tingle in her nose. She took another sip. Even more of a mystery, who was her father? A blue-blood pretty-boy amusing himself while waiting for his trust fund to kick in? A greaser from the wrong side of the tracks? Was he Anglo-Saxon? Italian? Japanese?

"I'm just a mutt," she mumbled. "Origin unknown. A mutt who can't keep her legs together . . . just like her mother. Trouble . . . always in trouble."

She closed her eyes and pushed her head against the scratchy wool pillow as the plane thundered on.

༄

Her childhood in Murray had been, by all appearances, idyllic. She'd spent her summers frolicking in the woods from sunup to sundown, her skin redolent with pine sap and the sweet scent of adventure and her face perpetually tanned. Inevitably, the aspen leaves would turn and fall, smothering her world in a riot of gold, a rustling sea for her to shuffle through on her way to the quaint, four-room schoolhouse in town. There, squeezed between bouts of reading and math, she'd learned the niches and blocks of social order, defended herself in the first and only fistfight she would ever experience, and grew some sense of who she was. Winters were a long, cold walk of frozen breath and Christmases. Seasons passed until she was no longer a child, and life was a cycle of happy norms.

Looking back, she saw the chips in the glossy veneer, gaps she had felt even as a child. There were long silences between her parents and a chill apathy in her father's attention. Attention that too often manifested itself in temper. She realized, too late, that this hurtful absence had helped drive her into Rick's arms. As she grew into a pretty, sharp-tongued teenager, the boredom of her tiny world and unvarying circle of acquaintances had rubbed a blister of wanderlust on her soul and raised an unexpected streak of rebellion in her.

What was there to do in a place like Murray but get into trouble? She could still feel the sting of the wind on her face and the slap of wayward branches as she barreled down the mountain on top of his van, whooping and hollering as she cheated death for a cheap thrill. Later, they'd holed up in the back with a fifth of stolen vodka and a six-pack of cheap beer to while another Friday night away. She'd heard the rustling of the pines outside his bedroom window, the hiss of the cold wind in the trees, as she searched for love and meaning in his arms, and scant weeks later she had known. She had known with a certain dread, an intuition that didn't need proof. She'd taken the test anyway and hid the results beneath her mattress for a week, wondering whom to tell first.

Rick had taken the announcement of his progeny better than she'd expected, kept the cursing to a minimum and nonchalantly offered to make an honest woman out of her as soon as he could get some new shoes. The offer, while not the bent-kneed declaration of undying love she had always envisioned, seemed heartfelt. Emily realized later that she had married Rick not out of some misconception of love or even duty, but because she thought it would impress, or at least mollify, her father. They were married three weeks later by a judge in Denver who kept the ceremony short. Rick had beamed in a natty new suit, and Emily couldn't help but wonder which he was more excited about that day: his bride or his wardrobe. Her face had burned when the judge called two strangers in from the hall to serve as witnesses. No family or friends had stood by their side for the momentous occasion, just an old woman, half blind beneath the fluorescent lights, and a punk from the local community college who'd stared at her neck the whole time. Rick's parents hadn't been pleased with his decision, and wouldn't come. Her father had declined the invitation; the shop was particularly busy on Saturdays, and one of the new machines had been acting up. She would have rather he yelled, would have preferred him to stomp and rage and call her a whore, to tell her she had ruined their good name, that her child would be born in sin, all the things she'd told herself. Anything would have been better than his detached reasoning. It made her feel like a wisp of fog on a cold morning, like she hardly existed at all.

They'd spent their first night as man and wife in Rick's basement bedroom, the same room that had brought them to grief in the first place. It all looked so different in the light of day, she'd thought as she dashed to the bathroom the next morning to empty her stomach. Eventually, they'd found a trailer on the edge of town, and Rick had taken a job as a line cook at the Murray City Diner. He'd dutifully brought his share of the tips home after every shift, dumping them on the kitchen table for Emily to count while Jericho gurgled her delight at the clatter of the coins. They'd saved enough by their second anniversary to buy a tiny house in the trees, closer to town, where Jericho learned to walk, weaving around furniture in the living room while Emily applauded. It was also where her daughter had learned life's most important lesson, in Emily's mind: Never trust a man.

Rick, her husband of three years, father of her only child, had left for the diner one morning with a strange new light in his eyes. She'd watched him walk away, picking a straight path through the trees, and waited for him to turn around and give her a wink or blow her a kiss. He'd never looked back.

"Daddy's gone," Jericho would chatter from her high chair. "Daddy's gone."

For love of his granddaughter, John Blyton had taken them in. Emily had defaulted on the cabin in the woods, weeping more over this loss than over the divorce papers. John had dutifully tucked Jericho in each night as Emily donned her ruffled apron and forced a smile for her job as a waitress at the seedy Black Bull Tavern. After a year of serving stale food to the beer-swillers perched at the bar, she'd found a job manning the register in one of the art galleries on Main Street and moved out of her father's house for the second time. The owner of the gallery was an older woman who understood the rocky road of single motherhood, having raised two boys on her own after her husband died in the mines. Jericho could stay at work with Emily, Merle had said, as long as she didn't deter customers. On the contrary, tourists had been drawn to the little girl's brown curls and shy smile as she bounced on her mother's lap behind the counter, and by the end of the first month Merle had given Emily a raise.

Jericho had loved the lofty gallery and spent countless happy hours studying the artwork on the walls or scribbling her own on sketchpads donated by Merle, who'd slipped her a fat, fresh book every few months.

"Keep at it, dear," she always said with a wink. "There's an artist in you somewhere, just trying to get out."

Emily had vowed not to repeat her father's mistake and had showered affection on her daughter in the best way she knew how: instruction. She'd carefully imbued Jericho with every drop of wisdom wrung from her own misguided life, desperate to give her a fighting chance at something better. Jericho had borne it admirably until she turned fourteen, when a wrathful creature with a bottomless well of bitterness had emerged, like some horrible monster springing from its cave after years of hibernation. Emily had picked her battles, giving her daughter the space every teenager craved. In hindsight, she knew it wasn't space that Jericho had wanted, but intimacy.

I did the best I could. She didn't exactly make it easy.

⚜

Two more drinks and seemingly days later, they reached New York. Emily let out a yelp as the plane hit the runway with a thump that she swore signaled the death throes of the wounded bird. She tottered into LaGuardia and collected her bags. *What now?* Her temples beat through a muddled fog. She would find somewhere to stay. A dark room and a decent bed. Her address book weighed heavily in her purse as she hailed a cab. Jericho's number was inside the front cover. A familiar, if not friendly, face and a place to stay were one phone call away. She would call Jericho tomorrow, Emily told herself, she didn't want to impose.

On the advice of her gregarious cabbie, she found a reasonable three-star hotel on the West Side and collapsed into bed, hoping as she slid from consciousness that she'd given him enough of a tip.

⚜

Jericho Hadden picked at the pile of noodles on her plate, her gaze drifting past the windows and into the perfect summer night beyond. The city was tossing its hair in the breeze, scenting the world with the promise of fleeting warmth as autumn closed in. In the park across the street, clots of old men huddled around their chessboards in the failing light, ignoring the young terrors who zipped past on skateboards and blades. A couple canoodled under an awning in nauseating bliss. Jericho sighed and mashed a noodle between the tines of her fork.

It had been an unsettling day, the kind that even Thai food and ginger tea in her favorite booth at her favorite restaurant were hard-pressed to erase. Things had started off well, all sunshine and blue skies streaming through the skylights at the art gallery where she worked, but had taken a turn for the worse with an innocent comment from a customer after lunch. Jericho had been wrapping an oversized print of Central Park for an elderly gentleman when she noticed two women intently absorbing a collection of paintings. They exchanged murmurs and nods as they traced the lines of color in the air.

"Do you think this place really exists?" one asked.

Jericho stopped wrapping.

"I don't know, but it's beautiful," the other replied. "The artist obviously feels deeply for it. Look at the care of the brushstrokes here."

The rest of the conversation had been lost on Jericho as the women marveled over her depictions of life in Murray.

Of course she felt deeply about that place. It was her home. It was only natural that it would have a voice in her work. She went back to wrapping, taping paper around the corners of the print with a mindless vigor. The problem was, Murray was the only voice in her work. Try as she might, she couldn't paint anything else with the same fervor that she

painted the snowy peaks and wildflowers of home. The paintings sold well in the little gallery, and her boss always gave
her a corner to display her latest creations, but her inability to
break free of her home and her mother taunted her like a fresh
breeze through a barred window. Worse yet, she reached for
the phone like one of Pavlov's slobbering hounds whenever
she dwelt on Murray for too long. Even now, her fingers rested
on the receiver.

"What am I doing?"

Call her.

The usual excuses came to roost around her. *I'm at work.
Personal calls are totally unprofessional.* The bells above the
door jangled as the women left. The gallery was empty. *It's
long distance. I don't have that kind of*

"Yes, I do. I have plenty of money."

I'm sure she's busy. She's not going to want to hear from me.

Her mother's last email came to mind, cautiously friendly
with an ill-disguised undercurrent of desperation. *I miss you,*
it had ventured, *please call.*

Her only excuse involved avoiding the awkward silences
that punctuated their conversations, and that excuse was just
a sign of weakness. Besides, her fingers, slender and betraying, were already dialing the number she had tried so hard to
forget. One ring. Two. Jericho pressed her hand to her chest to
still the strange beating of her heart. Three rings. Any moment
now, her mother would answer. They would talk about everything and nothing, and Jericho would feel like a daughter
again. Four rings. Five. An electronic chime sounded, and
Emily's voice filled the receiver, bright and recorded.

Jericho wilted, clicking off the phone in response to the
expectant beep on the other end.

Just like old times. Mom's never around.

She chided herself for being unfair. Emily had always been there for her, involved in every facet of her life. Always present, always loving, yet somehow . . .

"Inaccessible."

Jericho crossed the gallery to the wall where her paintings hung and ran her fingers over the dried oils, feeling suddenly tired.

"Where were you, Mom?" she whispered, her face inches from the paint. "All those years . . . you were holding out on me."

The sun shuddered from behind a cloud. Jericho stepped into the light, letting it gild her face with its mellow warmth. She still felt cold inside.

Jericho drifted back to the present and found a waitress at her side motioning with a pot of tea.

"Yes. Thank you," she murmured with a glance at her watch.

It was getting late. The lengthening shadows bled into darkness as headlights blinked on in the street, and a familiar cloud settled over her heart. Where was Mike? Had practice run late again? She could call him, but he wouldn't hear his cell phone over the squealing guitars and clashing cymbals anyway.

Speaking of inaccessible.

She considered herself to be an understanding girlfriend, more so than most, but sometimes Mike's schedule with the band was too much. And those girls, screaming and sighing at every concert as if he were Mick Jagger. She knew he was talented, but please. Jericho rubbed the bridge of her nose as she relived the awful awkwardness of yesterday, when she had offered him the spare key to her apartment. Mike had taken the key between his finger and thumb and dropped it into his pocket as if he thought it might explode, and when he'd told her he loved her it sounded like he was trying to convince himself.

Ten minutes later she was sure he had forgotten, again. She scrounged in her bag for a tip and walked home to her empty apartment alone, noodles and unshed tears solidifying in her stomach.

❦

Emily hovered at the cliff of a dreamless sleep, shuffling between her desire to plunge into oblivion and the necessity of rising. Her bladder pressed the necessity. A vague claw squeezed at the back of her skull, keeping time with her pulse. She groaned and opened one eye enough to find the bathroom. An apparition glared from the mirror. Swollen eyes, tangled hair.

I'm a vision of loveliness.

She needed her fraying bathrobe, a gallon of water, and another month to sleep off the hangover. Mercifully, the aspirin she'd packed was sitting open on the counter. She must have set it out last night, somehow knowing in her weepy state that she would need it in the morning.

Noise leaked into her room, cars squealing and roaring above the drone of a busy hive. She slipped on her sunglasses and peeked through the curtains, marveling at the surging mob on the sidewalk below. It was the entire population of Murray corralled within a couple of city blocks.

"This is where I was born?" she murmured, letting the curtain fall. "What have I gotten myself into?"

"Good morning!" a voice sang out behind her.

Emily whirled in a panic. Hadn't she locked the door? She had only been there one day, was she being mugged already?

92

"Welcome to New York!"

Emily staggered at the sight of a girl with a stack of fresh towels.

"I'm sorry. I didn't mean to startle you," the maid said. "I knocked, but no one answered."

"No, that's fine. Thank you for the towels." Emily grasped at her fleeing composure. "Please, come in," she finished awkwardly. The girl pulled the comforter over the bed and plumped the pillows with a practiced hand.

"First time in New York, huh?"

Emily nodded. "Is it that obvious?"

"Naw," the girl smiled. "You just have that look about you. You know, like you've never seen a skyscraper before."

Emily blushed. What was it about this city that left her so discomfited? She longed for the silence of the woods. All those people—it was a whole world beyond her grasp.

"Don't worry, people are friendly here." The maid emptied the trash and turned toward the door. "You'll do fine. Just keep an eye on your purse."

"Thanks," Emily called after her and sank onto the bed. She buried her face in her hands and waited for her stomach to unclench. "For what it's worth," she whispered, knowing it wasn't worth much, "I am Emily Blyton, and I'm not afraid."

Bolstered by a cup of coffee and a dry croissant, she slipped into the street an hour later, assaulted first by the smell of exhaust and the gritty warmth of the ubiquitous concrete, and second by the cacophony of the crowd. She wedged herself into a tide of people surging eastward and focused on the shoulders in front of her as bodies rolled by like rocks beneath a waterfall. It was Sunday, for pete's sake. Where were all these people going? Why weren't they snuggled under blankets at home or reading the paper on the couch or whipping up brunch for their neighbors at the kitchen counter? She drifted past a crowded bagel shop, envious of the easy laughter within, and slowly the blur of bodies around her came into focus. A family marched by in a bundle of happy children and balloons. Young men jostled each other and laughed their way up the street. A couple bickered bitterly at a streetlight, oblivious to anyone but themselves, as an elderly woman, impossibly tired, tottered through the crosswalk to a symphony of horns. A middle-aged executive straightened his tie and grinned at her as he passed, and she thought instinctively of Stanley. People were people, it seemed, wherever you went.

She wondered what Jericho was doing. Working? Sleeping in? Bad-mouthing her mother to sympathetic friends? She needed to find her daughter. She couldn't come all the way to New York, the very place Jericho had chosen for a home, and not contact her. What kind of mother would do such a thing? Someone jolted into Emily from behind, and she stumbled forward, grasping the jacket in front of her for support.

"Excuse me," she murmured. "I'm so sorry."

Why was their relationship so touchy? She never knew what would set Jericho off, sometimes nothing more than a word or a look. What if she showed up on her daughter's doorstep, only to have the door slammed in her face? Emily didn't think she could handle that kind of rejection at the moment. Then again, wasn't cold rejection what Jericho was always accusing her of?

⊸✿⊶

"What do you care?" a fourteen-year-old Jericho sneered in her memory. "You don't care what happens to me."

94

"Honey, you know that's not true. Don't say such hurtful things."

The angry imp, blossoming into a taller, darker version of her mother, stamped her foot.

"Then why won't you let me go see Daddy in Florida?" she demanded. "He's only going to be there a week, and he said I could come." Her grey eyes clouded like snow rolling in over the mountains. "You're just jealous," she hissed. "You don't want me to know my father because you're afraid I'll love him more than you."

In truth, Rick's birthday card to Jericho, one of the few he'd remembered to send over the years, had contained a casual mention of his upcoming trip to a friend's summer home on the beach and a vague pleasantry that she should come out sometime. Not exactly a solid invitation. If Emily knew her ex correctly, he would be surprised and mildly disappointed by the unexpected arrival of his teenage daughter. A week of neglect would follow, and Jericho would be shipped home early in tears, shredded self-esteem and mildewed duffle bag in tow. Emily hadn't known how to express her fears to her daughter, so she didn't. She'd reverted to the timeless mantra of "I'm your mother, and I know what's best," which met with a shriek, an accusation of cruelty, and a slammed door. Jericho's piercing eyes, glittering with furious tears, still sliced like a wet blade through her memory.

⁂

A large woman stamped on her foot. Emily yelped in surprise.

"Watch it!" she snapped, yanking her foot away like a wolf from a trap. The woman murmured an apology, cheeks flushed, as she turned away. "Wait!" Emily shrieked over the bobbing heads. "I'm sorry."

The woman had vanished from sight. Emily went limp. Maybe she was better suited to the city than she thought. Suddenly, it was all too much. The marching bodies with their sharp voices and myriad offensive smells turned her stomach. She limped toward a side street, a lonely woman about to puke in the gutter.

What's wrong with me?

What had happened to her neatly ordered world? Sure, it had been based on a secret, on a lie, but it had worked. Ignorance was bliss.

The sun finally slivered through the clouds in a needle of silver light. Across the street, an enormous flower burst forth from its stone setting, casting puddles of color on the sidewalk.

"How beautiful," she breathed, walking toward the intricate stained glass. It was the most beautiful piece she had ever seen, with winding vines and golden crowns. Emily climbed the steps of the church for a closer look.

She slipped into a corner at the back of the massive sanctuary, thoroughly modern but for the gorgeous stained glass, and sat agape at the crowd. How many people were there? A thousand, maybe? More? Struck by the horrible thought that perhaps she had interrupted a funeral, Emily craned her neck to survey the front of the room. No coffin, thank God, just a tall, sandy-haired fellow with a Bible in his hand. He reminded her of Ian, though his face was different, and Emily felt a stab of longing for her friends and her home.

"Some of you here this morning may feel like you don't belong." His quiet voice pierced her thoughts. "You may feel that you don't have many friends. That you're alone in the world, unsure of how you fit into it. Unsure of who you even are."

Emily stiffened. Was this some kind of joke? Was he one of those preachers who preyed on the emotionally distraught, promising fulfillment if only they would donate a hefty sum?

"The Bible says that God is a Father to the fatherless. That He puts the lonely into families, and provides for the orphans and the widows. That He knows every detail of your life and every hair on your head."

Emily rose from her seat and made for the exit. The last thing she needed was false comfort. An emotional crutch, that's all it was.

"Daughter," the pastor whispered. Emily went cold. "You are precious to me."

The world was suddenly still. She sprouted roots in the carpet, scarcely able to breathe as the crowd stood for a final song. It was as if the voice of God Himself had found her. What was that he'd said?

"Daughter," she said under her breath.

A hand thrust into her space. It was the pastor, smiling in tan trousers and a polo shirt.

"I'm Paul," he said. She squirmed. What had she done to attract his attention? Had he seen her trying to leave? "I hope you enjoyed the service."

She shook his hand dumbly, wondering what was wrong with her eyes. Those weren't tears, were they? She dropped his hand and dashed the moisture from her cheeks. He was still smiling pleasantly, waiting for her to speak.

"I'm Emily. Yes." She groped at the chair behind her. "Thank you. That last part was particularly moving." What was she saying? The last thing she wanted to do was encourage the guy.

He nodded. "It's comforting to remember that we have a heavenly Father who knows us."

"Sure." Emily forced a smile. "If you'll excuse me." She darted for the exit, grateful for the concealing crowd.

Outside, she burst into the street like a shipwreck survivor feeling sand between her toes. What was her problem? The first time in her adult life she darkened the door of a church, and she ended up in tears? Was she losing her mind?

"It's jet lag," she gasped, pounding the pavement back to her hotel. "It's this whole adoption mess. I'm just feeling a bit fragile."

People believed what they needed to believe. Whatever got them through another day. She could understand how the whole religion idea was appealing, she grudgingly admitted as she turned a corner and pushed through the jostling crowd. It gave a sense of meaning to otherwise meaningless lives, an identity to an orphaned society. What was it Marx called it? The opiate of the masses? After all, who wouldn't want some great, benevolent father watching over her with rapt attention?

"Too bad," she sighed. "Fathers like that just don't exist."

❦

Back at the hotel, Emily smiled politely at the bellboys and front-desk clerks, shot a friendly wave to her maid, emerging from the linen closet with fluffy towels piled up to her chin, and tried to convince herself that she wasn't desperately lonely. It was Sunday afternoon, a time for long walks in the woods and watching football games with friends, and she was stuck in a strange city with nary a tree or neighbor in sight. She bought a magazine at the newsstand in the lobby and headed for the hotel bar, determined not to mope in her room for the remainder of the day. After a lite beer and three articles detailing the unsatisfactory sex lives of housewives, her eyes began to droop. The padded mock leather of the booth cradled her head as she sank into a dim corner of memory.

※

"Emily!" her father barked. "Get in here." Emily had learned by the mature age of eleven how to decipher his various tones, which ranged from mild irritation to calculated disappointment, with some certainty. "Now!"

She scurried to the garage, composing an apology for the unknown offense. If he would just listen.

"What is this?" He motioned, larger than life, to a series of purple spatters across the floor of his workshop. She followed the line of paint across the concrete.

"I'm sorry. I was working on something for school. For my art class. It's just watercolor paint, I can . . ."

The back of his hand forced the breath from her mouth.

It didn't really hurt, she realized distantly, fighting for balance. It wasn't meant to hurt, but to shame. Hot tears bobbled at her lower lashes. She tucked her chin and let her hair fall around her face.

He swore under his breath.

"Stop your blubbering," he grunted. Was that his attempt at comfort? "Clean this up and help your mother with dinner." He disappeared in a blur of denim and boots as the tears charged past her nostrils and over her lip.

Her mother found her scrubbing at the clean concrete an hour later, hiding out in the garage until her tears subsided.

"Dear," she gathered the forlorn girl into her arms, "he means well. He just wants the best from you."

Emily turned and wept into her mother's neck. She didn't know, Emily was sure of it. Mother didn't know the extent of his temper, that he hit her sometimes. But what could Emily say? Her mother was a wisp of cloud, graceful and insubstantial. She had learned to stay ahead of the storms her husband brought home.

"He doesn't love me," Emily whimpered.

"He does love you," Mother soothed. "You know how Daddy is. He just likes everything to be a certain way. He wants things how he wants them."

"What if I can't be what he wants?" It was her greatest fear. His disappointment circled her like a shark sniffing for wounds as she floundered through life.

"Shhh. You're perfect." Mother patted her back. "You're perfect. You're very precious to us."

"Why can't he tell me that?" she sobbed. "Why? Is there something wrong with me?"

"No, baby." Mother rocked her gently on the floor until she fell asleep.

⁓✵⁓

Emily woke with a start, cheek pressed into the plastic of the booth, and looked around furtively. Thank goodness the bar was almost empty. She wiped her hand across her mouth reflexively, smoothed her shirt, and slid from her seat with one last glance around.

"Precious," she muttered as she rubbed her tingling legs and slunk toward the elevators. "What a crock."

E I G H T

I'VE never seen so many books!" the woman exclaimed, staring at the shelves with her mouth agape. "Honey, have you ever seen so many books?"

The man beside her patted her hand. Emily thought he looked a little embarrassed. His wife chattered on, a middle-aged Tinkerbell awash in a fairy world of wonder, while he discreetly pried her fingers from his jacket.

Geez, Emily thought, *that's not what I look like, is it?*

A scant four days in New York, and she was already finding her feet, praying she didn't look like a tourist as she pounded the pavement with every scrap of confidence she could marshal. She glanced back at the woman and hid a smile behind the book in her hands. The library was amazing, she had to concede. Row upon row of massive shelves reached up to the lofty ceiling and made Emily feel like a little girl again, wandering in the forest far from home.

"I wonder how many trees it took to fill these shelves," she muttered as she ran her fingers from one smooth spine to the next. "Or how many people have touched these same books over the years."

She paused at a yellowed volume of poetry. Maybe her own mother, her own father had once held that book. She slid it from the shelf. As she turned the pages, a loose page popped from the crumbling binding and fluttered to the floor.

"O My Luve's like a red, red rose, / That's newly sprung in June," she read as she stooped over the page. Had her father used such words to woo her mother? Had he wined her and dined her until she, caught in the raptures of romance, had yielded her virtue? Or had she been looking for love all along, mistaking groping affection for something unconditional? Maybe her own father—Emily's grandfather—hadn't really loved her. Maybe in desperation she had given everything she had to feel wanted, even just for a moment. To feel like she belonged, for once in her life, to someone or something other than herself.

"Can I help you, ma'am?"

Emily slipped the book back onto the shelf and turned to the uniformed young man beside her.

"I'm sorry," he smiled. "I thought you might be looking for something specific." Emily glanced at his nametag.

"No, thank you . . . Jack." She smiled back. "I'm fine." The words were out before she could review them, and as she watched him disappear toward the periodicals, Emily wanted to wring her own neck. Would she never learn to ask for help?

"Wait!" She ran after him. "I'm trying to research a genealogy," she blurted. "Where would be a good place to start?"

❦

Emily leafed through what seemed like the hundredth drawer of birth certificates with a sigh. Two hours and a dozen paper cuts later, she wasn't any closer to the truth. *What did you think? That it would fall into your lap? These things take time.*

"And digging." She sighed. "Lots of digging."

It would help if she knew her mother's first name. Already she had unearthed five female Tilbergs, none of whom had been born in Manhattan in the right time frame. Maybe Harry had been wrong. Hadn't he said he'd pieced together the information from her father's drunken ramblings? She shook her head and filed another record neatly in its drawer. No, Harry was too careful, too particular about the details of life for that. If there was anyone she could trust, it was him. A wave of loneliness assaulted her. Everyone in the world who cared at all about her was very far away. She dabbed at her eyes and fought a prick of self-pity. What a ninny she was becoming.

Suddenly, as if in answer to her emptiness, a laugh rang out over the bookshelves. Emily froze, breath stalled in her lungs and Kleenex crumpled in her hand. It couldn't be. There were eight million people in the city . . . eight million. A warm chuckle wafted through the books, mirthful and teasing and utterly unique.

"Jericho," she whispered.

Emily hovered, torn between two impulses. Finding her daughter would require her to autopsy her past before she was ready, but walking away from her child, so warm and bright and living, was something she couldn't do. Emily rose and followed the sound.

She wove between the wheeled carts of books, turned the corner, and found herself face-to-face with an empty table. She tried to feel relieved. Jericho would have been upset that she hadn't told her she was in town.

"Mother?"

Emily turned. Why couldn't her daughter just call her "Mom," like every other daughter on the planet? Jericho stood rooted to the carpet. Her purse had fallen to the floor, and Emily fought the urge to tell her to pick it up. This was New York, after all. Jericho stepped closer, searching Emily's face for some sign that she wasn't dreaming.

"What—" She dropped the hand of the young man at her side and lowered her voice. "What on earth are you doing here?"

Emily took her daughter in with one hungry glance: brown hair with a red sheen, grown longer than she remembered; piercing eyes, more gray than blue; stylish, sophisticated, utterly different, yet always the same.

"Jericho," Emily whispered. She forced a smile. "How have you been, dear?"

Jericho looked at a loss for words, and Emily was shocked again by the gross hilarity of the situation. Her daughter had been no doubt living her life to the fullest, rarely wasting a thought on her mother, when Emily materialized out of thin air, expecting a happy reunion.

"Fine, Mother. I'm doing fine," Jericho said, picking up the cue that this was not going to be a normal conversation. "Um, Mother, this is Mike." She motioned behind her. Mike nodded politely and held out his hand.

"Hello," he said. Emily shook his hand. Behind them, friends met with a warm embrace, and Emily was suddenly embarrassed by her daughter's civility.

"Seriously, what brings you to New York?" Jericho asked.

Emily cleared her throat. How would her daughter react to the news? Could she somehow cushion the blow? *Remember Grandma and Grandpa? They weren't really yours . . . I've dis-*

covered that we're genetic anomalies . . . remember how you
always wanted to be a princess? Who knows, you might be one
after all.

She couldn't tell her. Not here. Not like that.

"I, uh, I found a buyer here . . . in New York . . . who wants
a window. You know, one of those intricate custom deals." She
cleared her throat. "Anyway, he flew me out here to look at
some designs."

"You weren't even going to call me, were you?" Jericho
was emotionless. Mike shifted uncomfortably behind her and
turned his attention to a book. "Didn't even want to see your
own daughter. But then, you never were the motherly type."

Emily embraced the barb, tucking it under her heart as she
had learned to do long ago.

"Jericho, it's not like that. This came up suddenly. It was a
last-minute thing, you know? I just got here on Saturday."

"Oh," Jericho said flatly. "Well, I don't want to get in your
way." She softened, blurted, "If you need a place to stay, I
have a couch."

Emily blinked. Her daughter's unexpected kindness was
too much to take in.

"I wouldn't want to impose," she mumbled. "I already
found a hotel."

"Fine." Jericho pursed her lips. Emily stepped back. Was
that hurt in her daughter's eyes? "You've got my address if
you change your mind." Jericho turned and disappeared. Mike
looked up, startled, from his book.

"It was very nice to meet you," he offered as he left.

They bolted for the stairs, and Emily was tempted to let
them go. But hadn't that always been the pattern? Emily
would somehow say all the wrong things, Jericho would spit
glass before listening to what Emily was really trying to say,

and they would part ways, hurting and hateful and always alone. Emily turned, heart on fire, and flew toward the stairs.

"Wait!" she yelled. "Come back here—" *Young lady.* "Jericho! Please wait. We need to tal—" She turned a blind corner and barreled into Jericho. Emily stumbled backward and sat down hard on the step behind her. She picked herself up, desperate to glean some scrap of dignity from the situation, but unwilling to let her daughter go.

"Ow! Mom, let go of my arm."

"Jericho, please don't run away. I'm sorry I didn't tell you I was coming to New York," she panted. "I was afraid you'd be angry. It's just that you're always upset with me, and I—"

"So it's *my* fault?" Jericho screeched. "I am not having this conversation!" She started down the stairs again with Emily at her heels.

"Stop it!" Emily hissed, grabbing at her daughter's arm in vain. Jericho jerked her sleeve from Emily's grasp, and they tumbled out the door onto the sidewalk like a pair of injured hornets. Jericho spun toward the street, her heels clicking angrily through the crosswalk as the light changed.

"Jericho! Wait, please wait," Emily called, weaving through the traffic to the sound of blaring horns. She gained the sidewalk on the other side, grateful for her life, and cast about for a tumble of coppery hair. She caught sight of Jericho a block away, loping along at a furious pace.

What if I had a heart attack right here on the sidewalk? What if I was hit by a cab? She wouldn't even care.

The thought was maddening, and Emily went momentarily limp before adrenaline surged into her veins. She hadn't been so angry since . . . since Jericho left home. She chased after the vanishing form, pushing through the crowds, heedless of who saw her.

"Jericho!" she shrieked, and snatched the leopard-print purse from her daughter's hand with a lunge. Jericho stopped outside a bustling sidewalk café.

"What," she pushed between her teeth, "do you want, Mother?"

"Jericho, please," Emily gasped, clutching at her side, "I only came to New York to find my family."

"Your family! What am I?" Jericho yelled.

Emily wrangled for a breath as she shook her head.

"My real family, Jericho." Her hands began to shake. "Jericho, I was adopted."

A tremendous smash from inside the café sent waiters scrambling for cover as a tray of glasses tipped to the floor. Emily jumped back toward the street at the sound, but Jericho didn't blink.

"You're what?" Her eyes bored into Emily's.

"I was adopted, Jericho. I just found out."

"Great!" Jericho spat, throwing her arms into the air as she turned away. "That's just fabulous, Mom. First, I have no father and only half a mother. Now you're taking my grandparents from me?" She swore and stamped her foot. "I'm an orphan!"

Half a mother? Emily stepped back as if she'd been slapped. Tears wobbled from her eyes.

"No, honey," she whispered, "I am."

Jericho turned again and ran.

"Jer! Wait up!" It was Mike, charging after Jericho.

Emily didn't follow them.

Jericho wrapped her fingers around the mug, willing the warmth of the ceramic into her cold hands.

"C'mon, babe. That's like your third cup of tea. Are we going to be here all day?" Mike whined beside her.

"Just give me a minute," she whispered, wishing the tea would dissipate the cold fog around her heart. Patrons complained to the waitress at the counter behind her, and Jericho sighed. She hated to admit it, but New York would never be home. It was just too rough for her. Too gruff. Too loud. She missed the permeating stillness of the forest, the smell of granite in the sun.

Mike tapped irritably at a packet of sugar before tearing off the corner and dumping it onto the table.

"Why don't you get out of here," Jericho offered. "I know you've got things to do."

She would have preferred he stay and comfort her, but that was selfish, she supposed. Besides, after he had slipped her key back to her, thankfully without comment, there hadn't been much to say. He shrugged into his coat and dropped a kiss on the top of her head.

"I'll call you later," he said as he bolted for the door. Jericho sighed again as she watched him leave. If only she could understand what was bothering her. It wasn't just her mother, their fight, her startling news. There was a nameless and unfamiliar pain grasping at her heart that was too much to bear.

It wasn't . . . it couldn't possibly be.

"What do I have to feel guilty for?"

She wasn't the one who'd flown halfway across the country to her mother's home and hadn't bothered to tell her. She wasn't the one who had caused such a grievous rift in their relationship, who had always been aloof at the worst times, who'd hunkered in foxholes at the periphery of Jericho's life, leaping out to shoot pellets of advice when it was convenient.

Why did she always feel on guard with her mother? Why

couldn't she just be herself without the worry of what Emily would think or what she would say?

"It's like she lives in a jar."

The strange image assailed her as the mug slipped suddenly from her grasp and landed on the saucer with a clatter, launching tea over the edge.

Memories paraded past as she sat there, a captive audience with tea cooling on her pants.

She'd toted a book into her grandpa's lap. He had patted her head and asked Emily if she ever read to her daughter at home. Surely, she didn't want the child to turn out like— there'd been a calculated sniff—others they knew.

Emily had cut her finger while slicing bread.

"Always making trouble," Grandpa had intoned while Jericho colored nearby. "Why are you so clumsy?"

Thinking about it now, Jericho shuddered. Was every fond memory of her grandfather tainted with his cruelty to Emily? What must her mother's life have been like with that man?

"No wonder," she whispered.

The waitress grumbled as Jericho bolted for the door.

❧

Wandering back to the hotel that night, Emily had the strange desire to go on a bender. She had never been much of a drinker, not since the wild oat-sowing days of her youth, but lately the oblivion of a soused stupor was becoming increasingly appealing. She clapped a hand over her mouth at a sudden thought. What if alcoholism ran in her family? A parade of imaginary uncles, cousins, even her own mother, staggered past, raising their glasses to her. The desire for a drink shriveled and died with the thought, and she pressed on, vowing never to touch the stuff again.

Maybe it was time to go home. She was becoming too familiar with New York. Somehow, the city brought out the worst in her, her ugliness pushing to the surface like blood beneath a bruised nail. Besides, her quest was proving fruitless, and her presence in the city was only causing her daughter pain. Jericho, who hardly acknowledged her own mother, who deserted Emily for a fling in the city, then complained of the distance between them . . . who sat curled up in the hallway with her back to Emily's door.

"Honey?" Emily crept from the elevator, barely trusting her own eyes. Jericho trembled and flicked a tear away with her thumb. "Baby, what is it?" Was she hurt? Had she been attacked? Lost her job? Her apartment? Her boyfriend? Emily sank to her knees and brushed a lock of hair from Jericho's face. Jericho looked up with a watery grimace.

"Sorry," she whispered.

"What for? I'm the one who—"

"No." She pulled Emily's hand from her face. "Let me say this. I'm sorry I flipped out back there. I felt hurt that you didn't tell me you were coming. That you didn't want to stay with me." She sniffed. "But I didn't even give you a chance to explain. I mean, no wonder you didn't want to tell me. Look at the way I reacted." Her hands flopped to her side.

Emily fought the impulse to ask for the apology in writing. She could frame it . . . hang it in the living room.

"Mom?"

"Sorry. I was just thinking," Emily smiled. "If the offer's still open, I'd love to stay with you."

Jericho nodded.

"I'd like that. But why didn't you want to stay with me in the first place?"

"I don't know." Emily leaned against the wall. "I didn't want to cramp your big-city lifestyle."

Jericho rolled her eyes until Emily swore she was looking at her own brain.

"That's such an excuse."

Emily sank to her knees. What kind of woman was afraid of her own daughter? *She doesn't let me hide.*

"You're right," she said. "That's an excuse. I didn't tell you I was coming because I was afraid you'd slam the door in my face."

Jericho nodded, taking it in.

"I'm sorry. I probably have slammed a lot of doors on you over the years."

Emily nodded mutely. She knew how much the admission must have cost her daughter.

"I'm sorry too," she whispered. "For so much."

Jericho wrangled in her pocket for a key and handed it to Emily.

Emily took the key, grateful for small blessings.

"I'll check out in the morning," she said. "Thank you."

⚜

That night Emily struggled through restless dreams, empty, dark, and exposed, and woke the next morning in a cloud. How could last night's joy evaporate so quickly? She thought of the hummingbirds that flocked through Murray in the spring and summer months, tiny jewel-toned warriors thrumming and jostling for a place at someone's feeder, battling for a little more of the ruby sweetness that kept them alive.

Eventually the nectar ran out, and they were left threading desperate beaks into an empty tube.

Emily fluffed the pillows wearily and left a tip for the maid beneath the lamp before she realized that the maids would need to strip the sheets from the bed she had just made. A creature of habit, that's all she was, a miserable creature of habit. How long had she been running on instinct? Going through the motions so she wouldn't have to think? She flung open the drapes, soaking her face in the punishing light.

What was she doing here, clinging trembly lipped and teary eyed to the windowsill of a strange place?

Looking for him.

The thought wafted past her like a cobweb.

But what good would it do? What good could possibly come of finding the father who hadn't cared enough to keep her? Did she really think she was going to confront him? What on earth would she say?

"I'm the daughter you wish you'd never had, you jerk."

Nothing would suffice. Was there anything she could say to him, anything he could say to her, that would fill the void in her heart?

"I'm proud of you," she whispered, letting the light stream over her hair and her face. "I've always loved you."

She closed her eyes and remembered.

"And the first-place ribbon goes to . . ."

The suspense was unbearable. Sixty first-graders writhed in unison as the ribbons for the annual spelling bee were awarded.

"Emily Blyton! Emily, come here, dear."

The principal coaxed her to the front of the gymnasium and pinned the silky strip of blue to her dress.

"We're all very proud of you," she said.

Emily beamed.

The bell signaled the end of another school day. She rushed out to the sidewalk with the others, fluffing her hair and her collar and the ribbon all the way home.

"Mom will be so proud," she said to the ribbon. "And Dad . . . he'll be proud of me too."

She could almost see the gleam of satisfaction in his eyes. He would pat her on the back, holding the ribbon up to the light to see it shine.

She skipped up the steps to her house.

Maybe he would even brag to his friends at work about how smart his daughter was.

"Emily."

She skidded to a halt in the entryway before her father, thrusting her shoulder forward to help the ribbon catch the light.

"What is that?"

"I won first place in the spelling bee," she whispered.

"What happened to your dress?"

Emily looked down. The heavy ribbon had torn the lace of her collar.

"You're just determined to make as much work for your mother as possible, aren't you?"

She bowed her head.

"Take that off now." He plucked at the ribbon and tossed it onto the coffee table. "No one likes a show-off."

She made her way to her bedroom, heart withering like a little brown leaf, and sat on the edge of her bed. She was beginning to understand. She was on her own.

Thirty-five years later, in a hostile city and a sterile room, she refused to cry.

It was his loss.

A precious little girl he never knew.

His loss.

Emily pressed her face to the glass. She could almost smell the concrete, slowly disintegrating beneath the endless tread of feet, and the tarred streets baking in the sun.

It's my loss.

"God!" She slapped the glass with her open palm and cursed. "Why do I need a father?"

Slap.

"Why do I care?"

Emily whirled from the window and grabbed her bag. It was a question she couldn't answer. Not yet.

"Check out by eleven," she muttered and headed for the door.

NINE

SUZANNA Tilberg stirred to the sound of laughter. Her arm, pinned beneath her body, wouldn't respond. What time was it? She pried open her eyes. Faint sunlight lit her bedroom curtains from behind.

"It's Saturday," she grumbled, scrounging for her slippers beneath the bed. "Don't these kids ever sleep?"

She rounded the corner to the kitchen, pushing tangled hair from her face, and paused at the scene before her. The twins, Ruth and Jordan, cracked eggs into a mixing bowl. Will, slightly older and therefore capable of handling greater responsibility, beat the batter solemnly with a whisk. Samantha poured orange juice into glasses on the counter, and Janice—bless her heart for working at Hope House—Janice supervised the whole procedure. Suzanna smiled.

"What are you guys doing up so early?" she yawned. "It's Saturday."

Someone thrust a mug of coffee into her hand.

"We're making pancakes for everyone." Ruth beamed and wiped her hands on her shirt.

"Everyone" meant the eight other children currently residing at Hope House, who found themselves there because their parents were deadbeats, drug addicts, incarcerated, or some combination thereof—plus Janice and Suzanna, of course.

"Wow. That's a pretty big project." She smiled over her coffee at Janice. "But I'm sure everyone will love it. Mmmm." She made a show of leaning over the batter bowl. "Pancakes are my favorite."

Ruth beamed up at her while Janice discreetly picked eggshell out of the bowl.

"I'm going to grab a quick shower since you guys obviously have this under control," Suzanna said, "and then I'll wake everyone else up."

Quick was an understatement. With one rusting water heater of questionable age and fourteen individuals needing to bathe, showers over five minutes were a luxury. Suzanna pulled her mass of brown curls into a ponytail and tugged on her clogs. More voices joined the cacophony in the kitchen. From the exclamations of delight and the enthusiastic bickering over who got the syrup first, she could tell they were all awake. There was a moment of expectant silence as someone stumbled through a prayer, and then the forks began to fly.

Suzanna squeezed into a spot at the crowded table beside Janice. They were the skeleton crew, the only paid staff who lived with the children twenty-four hours a day, and as such they had become fast friends. Soon the daytime volunteers would join them, occupying the children for a few precious hours while Suzanna and Janice scheduled visits with social workers, applied for grants, and planned fund-raising events to keep the house afloat.

Suzanna's fork stopped halfway to her mouth.

"Zanna?" Ruth continued to chew as she spoke. "Don't you like the pancakes?"

Suzanna hurriedly finished the bite.

"I'm sorry, Ruth. They're wonderful. I was just thinking about everything I need to do today."

Janice nodded sympathetically.

"Is that grant still hanging over your head?"

"The deadline for proposals is Monday. I'm almost finished." Suzanna sighed. "Ten thousand dollars would buy a lot of pancake mix."

"New shoes, winter coats, and a new water heater," Janice smiled. "I was thinking about taking this mob to the zoo today. That would get us out of your hair."

"That," Suzanna savored another sugary bite, "would be wonderful."

Word of the zoo quickly spread the length of the table. Forks clanked double-time on plates as the children inhaled their breakfast and scampered off, squealing, for showers and fresh clothes.

"Wonderful," she whispered.

❧

An hour and two broken plates later, Suzanna sat propped at the head of her bed, making a mental note not to let Ruth dry the dishes without help next time while she stared at her dinosaur of a laptop. Too much of her education in raising kids was trial and error. She only hoped the children wouldn't suffer for it.

She was pecking out the last paragraph on why Hope House deserved that particular foundation's available funds more than any of the other desperate shelters in the city, when a knock sounded on the open door. That was Theodore, of course. He had asked permission to stay behind so he could finish the book he was reading. How could Suzanna say no?

"Come in, Teddy. You don't have to knock."

How could anyone say no to the quiet ten-year-old? He was small for his age, but cloaked in a studious confidence that often made him the reluctant leader of the group.

"Sorry to bother you." He shifted his book from one hand to the other and looked back at the door.

"You're never a bother. Come here."

Suzanna plopped the laptop none too gently beside her and made room for Teddy. He perched gingerly at the edge of the bed, examining her comforter as if it held the secrets of the ages.

"How did you like the book?"

He nodded, eyes still on the blanket. "It was good. The ending was pleasant yet unpredictable."

Suzanna allowed herself a small smile. He had been reading book reviews in the *New York Times* again. "Is there something else on your mind?"

Here Teddy shimmied uncomfortably, bunching the comforter in his fist. Suzanna waited. "Is my mom gonna come back for me?"

He launched the question forcibly and himself with it. Suzanna grabbed his wrist to keep him from falling.

Oh, dear.

These were the questions she hated. The desperate inquiries, framed beneath peaked brows, as to where a father was or when an aunt would be returning or, worst of all, why a mother had left. How was she to answer? How could she explain why some awful excuse for a parent had abandoned such a precious child in favor of a needle or a life of crime?

She cleared her throat. "I don't know, Teddy. I'm so sorry, I just don't know."

The brutal and awful truth. There was an endless debate among the social workers she knew as to which was worse: to allow children a peep at the cold, cruel world exactly as it was, or to trail them along on a fraying thread of hope until they were old enough to understand for themselves. It was an awful question without a decent answer.

She took his hand. "I wish I could tell you she was coming back." She wrestled for a moment with the knot in her throat. "We love you so much . . . Janice and I and all the others. You are so special to us. I don't know where your mom is or if she'll come back, but you'll always have a home here with us. We'll never leave you."

By the end of her wholly inadequate little speech, she was squeezing Teddy's hand like an orange she was trying to juice.

Teddy squeezed back as he weighed her words with solemn eyes. "Thanks."

He slid from the bed and vanished down the hall.

Suzanna flopped back onto her pillows and cried. The injustice of it all was just too much, and worst of all, she knew she would be hearing that question again.

TEN

EMILY slid the key Jericho had given her into the lock with a glance over her shoulder. How well did Jericho know her neighbors? Had she told them all about her nosy nuisance of a mother? After another fruitless day of scanning through microfiche in that endless cavern of a library, Emily was almost too tired to care. Almost. The bolt slid back smoothly. She opened the door.

"Hello?"

Jericho was at work, she reminded herself. It was silly, but she felt the need to announce herself to the cool, dark space. The first room was the kitchen. She fumbled for a light, banging her hip against the counter before she found the switch.

"Wow!" she breathed, massaging her leg. Somehow she'd expected the chaos and clothes explosion of Jericho's bedroom at sixteen. "Wow."

It was spotless. A lovely, tidy little space with soaring

ceilings and one open area that led into the next: a kitchen, a living room complete with worn but matching furniture, a tiny staircase, and a shadowed little loft where Jericho slept. Emily locked the door and dragged her suitcase into the living room.

"Oh, Jericho." Mountains ringed the walls, craggy and dusted with snow. "It's home!" Emily wanted to weep. Spring flowers trailed from window boxes and planters, a mountainside flamed forth in autumn glory, a woman stomped through the snow toward a friend, laughing as a dog charged ahead. A shaggy, red dog.

"I couldn't get away from it." Emily jumped at the sound of Jericho's voice in the doorway behind her. "I left Murray to find a bigger, better world," Jericho said, smiling sadly. "But all I can paint are the mountains. The summer storms." She laughed. "Old Harry and his walking stick."

Emily nodded.

"They're so beautiful." She bit back a flood of emotion. Jericho didn't need to see her blubbering like an idiot. "They make me feel like . . . like I haven't totally lost you."

A cloud passed over Jericho's face, a fleeting wisp of rain. She opened her mouth, then closed it again and turned to the fridge. She yanked it open, rummaging aimlessly.

"I got off work a little early so we could have dinner," she said, sniffing a carton of milk. "The couch is yours tonight, too, if you want it."

Emily turned to her luggage. What just happened, she wondered. A spark of something precious had died like a star dropping from the sky. What would it take for them to be friends?

"We can eat now if you'd like," Jericho offered nonchalantly. "But I'm going out tonight, so . . ."

Don't wait up, Emily filled in. How desperately did Jericho want to sneer those words?

". . . make yourself at home." Jericho smiled stiffly.

"I'd really like that." Emily chomped back the words of warning and turned back to the paintings in the living room. Her daughter's life was her own.

Jericho pulled her sweater over her head as she kicked off her boots. The change of clothes did nothing to strip off the guilt that draped around her like a robe.

"She's a grown woman," she muttered. "She's already spent several nights in this city by herself. It's not like she's helpless."

Still, what an awful way to treat a guest—her mother, no less. What kind of daughter was she?

"A busy one. My prior plans for the evening take precedence."

The jumble of hangers poking from her closet offered no assurance. She could easily duck out of dinner with her girl-friends or take Emily along. Instead, she was leaving her mother alone on what could have been their first night together in months.

She ran a brush through her hair and slipped into a jacket.

"Evil. I'm just evil."

I'm not ready for her. I'm just not ready.

It's my first night with her in so long.

A hot shower and the barren state of Jericho's fridge had coaxed Emily back into the city in search of dinner. Morose thoughts banged around inside her like the sneakers she had tossed into Jericho's washing machine before she left.

I can't believe she just took off. What happened to starting over? Being closer?

The sudden realization that she was the one who had come to New York with no plans of finding her daughter in the first place left a horrible taste in her mouth.

"Oh, God, what kind of terrible mother am I?"

The setting sun splintered over the windows of the office complex on her right, and as Emily turned she caught a glimpse of her face, weary and backlit by flaming orange.

"Her faults are my fault," she whispered to the reflection, longing to peer past the faint image in the glass to see who waited inside herself.

If only it were that easy.

She had never fully given herself to her daughter. No wonder Jericho was bitter.

"How could I? I never had myself to give."

A thin branch of thought sprouted from her memory. It was Jericho, sixteen and soaked to the bone, straddling her bedroom windowsill at two o'clock on a Sunday morning.

"Don't you remember what it was like to be young?" she had pleaded when Emily flipped on the light. "I'm sure you snuck out once or twice when you were sixteen."

"My past has nothing to do with your present." Emily had stabbed the point home with a finger in the air and watched her daughter wilt, dripping into the room. Jericho slid to the floor with a wounded look.

"Somehow I thought you'd understand," she had whispered, all streaming hair and big, dark eyes, and Emily *had* understood, but hadn't said so.

Now, Emily pressed her fingertips against the cool glass,

willing her image to speak, to give an answer. "My past has everything to do with her present. If only I knew what my past was."

Daughter, you are precious.

The thought assaulted her in a whisper, and Emily was suddenly furious with her own mind for betraying her. Lies! Whispered platitudes from some holy roller trying to prey on her emotions, nothing more. She swung away from the building. She didn't need a father, heavenly or otherwise. She had everything she needed in the neat, efficient package of herself. After all, who else could she trust?

No one. She clipped down the street, head up, shoulders back, defying any mugger to test her. Let them come. The world would see.

I can take care of myself.

Heavy music rubbed in the evening air. Raucous laughter leaked through the smoke-fogged windows of a corner bar covered with neon beer signs. Emily shivered, her bravado withering to her kneecaps. She had taken a wrong turn somewhere. Murray used to be filled with bars like that, years ago before the tourism boom, when only the faltering mines supported the town and the faltering miners still needed a place to unwind. They had traded the perpetual black of one cave for another every night, and Rick had joined them more often than not. In the throes of denial, Emily had kept her mouth shut as he picked through dinner before trudging off to the bar for good times and relaxation. She'd reminded him once that he wasn't even a miner, and asked how stressful being a line cook could be. It wasn't like he was in mortal danger every day. He had withered her with a glance. She didn't understand him at all, did she? She had no idea what his life was like, he'd said. She hadn't brought it up again. Until that terrible night.

What had started out as an afternoon of Jericho's run-of-the-mill fussing had burned into an evening of wailing and fever. Rick had taken the car, of course, and when Emily had called down to the bar, the owner told her she'd better come fetch him herself. She'd bundled Jericho in every blanket they owned and walked into town, praying that she wouldn't find him drunk.

He'd rolled a glassy eye her way as she crept up to the bar.

"Baby," he chortled, waving a bottle of beer expansively. "My baby's here."

He eyed the bundle in her arms.

"Both my babies. C'mere." He dragged her toward him. "Come sit . . . my lap."

Emily hung back in horror, eyes glued on the offending lap, where one of the waitresses from the diner already sat, her arm thrown around his neck and her curvy self pressed into his side. His hand slid lazily up her leg. Emily turned and fled.

"What?" he had yelled after her. "There's enough room!"

The memory faded, but the vision did not. Another young man, so much like Rick, stood pressed against a woman in the doorway of the New York bar. They swayed unsteadily as his hand crept down to the small of her back.

"Mike!" Emily gasped the name, then spun on her heel and fled, unwilling that Jericho's boyfriend should see her there. Her poor daughter, her poor deceived child. Maybe it was genetic, this knack for falling in love with losers.

Emily headed for the safety of Jericho's apartment, hunger forgotten.

"Do I tell her?" she moaned to the mirrored elevator as it hauled her to the fifth floor. Jericho's face hovered in her memory: eyes narrow, lips tight, as she spat out accusations of meddling and criticism. "I can't. I can't tell her. This is something she'll have to learn for herself."

The muzak crooned through a song Emily recognized, something about endless love. *Yeah, right.*

She stepped off the elevator and wandered toward Jericho's door. She fumbled at her purse, lost in the memory of Mike's roving hands.

"Stupid, stupid kid." She jammed the key into the lock. "He's giving up such a bright, beautiful—"

The door swung inward, catching Emily off-balance and catapulting her into the entryway.

"Mother."

Emily took in the ponytail, the sweatpants, and the nubby wool socks in a glance and panicked. Had Jericho somehow found out? She scrambled for a smile.

"Hi, honey. What are you doing home?"

"Honestly? I felt really bad about taking off like that. It's not that I don't want to spend time with you, it's just that . . . I don't really know how to."

"I know." Emily followed her inside. "I know."

Jericho had turned on the gas fireplace in the living room and set out two mugs of what smelled suspiciously like cocoa. Emily wrestled down a grin. Wasn't this the cozy, cliché mother-daughter friendship thing that Jericho had always railed against?

"What is it, Mom?"

"Your place is so inviting, honey. You've really made a nice life for yourself here."

"Thank you," Jericho beamed and handed Emily a mug. "So tell me what's been happening in Murray. Is Song holding up OK?"

Emily sank into the loveseat, joy pushing through her in a warm flood. She had dreamed about this moment for so long.

"Mom?"

Emily smiled and thought for one horrifying moment that she might weep. She closed her eyes.

"I'm just enjoying the moment, sweetie."

ELEVEN

BUG Mason roused from sleep at a whisper of a sound. She snuggled closer to Ian and tugged at the comforter with a grunt. It was almost September, for pity's sake. She didn't care that Murray was cradled in an unseasonably warm, dry fall; leaving the window open all night was still a bit ridiculous. Besides, those pine branches raking at the sill gave her the craziest dreams. She always seemed to be sweeping.

"Ian," she snuffled into his back. "Shut the window."

"Were you sweeping again?" he murmured and rolled over, taking the covers with him. Bug burrowed against his side and willed her mind to rest. It was a hazard of being a pastor's wife, she supposed. Sometimes the world was too much with her.

Ian began to jerk beside her in a series of shallow twitches that animated his legs and the length of his back. What was he dreaming of, she wondered. He always had the best dreams, and would undoubtedly recount this one for her and Grant over breakfast the next morning. She could almost picture him soaring over the woods and the mountains, propelled only by his arms and his will to fly, diving and looping through the blue, cloaked in the fragrance of the pines.

He stiffened beside her, the soft gravel of his breath suspended.

"Ian?" she whispered and put out a tentative hand.

He ejected from the bed like a pilot from a burning fighter jet, and roared, an indistinct, primal sound that propelled Bug to the other side of the room.

"Emily!" he screamed. "Run, Emily!"

He dove across the bed and landed in a heap near Bug, bashing his head against the side table. The lamp wobbled . . . wobbled . . . and fell with an anticlimactic crack against the hardwood floor.

Ian lay motionless. Bug trembled to his side.

"Oh, no," she breathed. "Ian, baby, are you OK?"

She ran her hands over his body, prodding for bruises or broken bones.

He groaned.

"Wake up, Ian." She tugged at his arm, "Wake . . . up."

"Where's Emily? Where is she?"

"She's in New York, sweetie, remember?"

"New York?"

He said it as if she had told him Emily was growing a third arm.

Oh, no, Bug thought, *he's finally lost it. Twenty years of ministry was too much for his poor mind.*

"Remember? She went to look for her family."

"I know, I know." He dragged himself back into bed and

hunched over his sheet-tented knees, rubbing the fresh knot on his head. "It was just so vivid."

"What?"

"A horrible, horrible dream."

There was a knock at the door, and Grant's tousled head appeared.

"You all right?" he asked, one arm jammed into the sleeve of a plaid robe.

"Yeah, we're fine," Ian said. "I just had a bad dream."

"Oh. I thought Mom had finally decided to kill you for leaving that window open."

"Go back to sleep, Grant. You look like a mole," Ian teased.

Grant grunted and trailed his robe back down the hall.

"Honey, what on earth were you dreaming about?" Bug kneaded at the small of his back.

"Emily and I were in the woods. We were looking for something . . . I don't know what . . . and it was hot and dark and there was something really bad coming. Just this sense of doom, you know. And suddenly I heard this huge crack, and I looked, and this huge, huge tree was falling. It was the biggest thing I had ever seen . . . I mean, it blocked out the sun. And it was falling right on top of her. I was screaming, but she wouldn't move. She just stood there looking at me like I was nuts. The tree kept falling, but I couldn't save her."

He shivered suddenly and slid to his knees beside the bed. "Pray with me, Bug. We need to pray for Emily."

"What's wrong?"

"I don't know, it just feels like she's in some kind of danger."

"What do you mean?"

"Don't be afraid. Just pray with me."

Bug knelt beside him, intertwining her fingers with his.

She followed the rise and fall of his voice as he petitioned the Almighty, her own thoughts mingling with his words.

Oh, God, keep her safe. Please watch over her. Don't let her be hurt.

TWELVE

"THIS," Jericho opened her arms, beaming with pride, "is where I work."

After an evening of fine wine and surprisingly pleasant conversation with her daughter at a charming corner bistro, Emily didn't know how things could get any better. She had almost cried when Jericho offered to give her a private tour of the gallery where she worked.

Thank goodness it's a reputable place, Emily thought as she took in the high-end studio. Jericho could make a living here.

"So, what do you think?" Jericho prodded.

"It's beautiful," Emily sputtered with relief. She didn't know why she had suffered for so long with visions of Jericho selling caricatures of dead presidents and celebrities from a kiosk on the street. Did she have so little faith in her daughter? "It's really gorgeous. Right up your alley, and I bet you're the best assistant manager they've ever had."

"Well, sales have increased since I've been here," Jericho smiled modestly. "And a lot of folks say the place has never looked better."

Emily followed the artwork around the walls. "I love how you've arranged the oil paintings. The progression of colors is fabulous. It really draws you in," she said.

Jericho glowed. "Let me show you my favorite." She ran to the back of the long room, and Emily couldn't help but see her little girl again, dark curls bouncing on her shoulders as she toddled off to find a picture in the gallery at home. "Here it is," Jericho held out the canvas carefully.

"Oohh, that's amazing," Emily breathed, reaching toward the rich colors. "That's really incredible."

"It's by a local artist. A guy who lives in the Village. I'm actually the one who convinced him to let us sell his work." She paused, and Emily sensed in the deliberate silence that she was trying to marshal fresh courage. "I'm going to buy it for Mike!"

"What?" Emily exhaled like a leaking tire. *For that philanderer?*

"It's three hundred dollars, but I've been saving for a while. I just know he'll love it."

Emily felt sick. Jericho's enthusiasm broke her heart, but if she said a word—a single word—about Mike, she would prove her daughter right. No, she wouldn't become the meddling control freak Jericho had always said she was. Not for the moment, at least.

"I'm sure he will," she managed to say.

⁂

Emily watched the clouds descend on the city, bulging with the promise of early snow. She zipped her jacket up to her chin with an envious glance at Jericho's soft scarlet scarf. Her daughter had a style all her own, Emily realized, and somewhere in the vibrant mess of the city and the life on her own, she had developed into a fascinating individual. Emily stuffed her chilled fingers into her pockets. Why couldn't she do the same? Why couldn't she move forward with her life, defining who she was by who she wanted to be? Why did it matter what her father, biological or otherwise, thought of her? She had proven to the world that she could make it on her own; why didn't she believe it herself?

Fog curled around the buildings like a gorged and sleepy snake. Emily pondered the question as timid flakes materialized against the black streets. It was the voice at the back of her mind, the voice second-guessing her every move, that made her so uncertain. *It's his voice.* She went weak at the thought. Hadn't she suffered enough of his criticism while he was alive? Was his disappointment going to haunt her forever? Emily decided then and there to keep her mouth shut about Mike. Jericho was a smart girl. In time, she would figure out the truth about her boyfriend. About all men.

"What is it, Mom?" Jericho broke the silence. "You look like you're about to burst."

Emily ran the tip of her tongue over her teeth. She willed the image of Mike and his bar-bunny from her mind, replacing them with a field of wildflowers. *Columbines . . . Indian paintbrush . . . wild roses dotting a mountain meadow.*

But the two of them were there, groping and moaning in the meadow with the roses at their feet. His hands slid down her back toward the point of no return. Emily seethed. The flowers vanished.

"I don't think you should buy that painting for Mike."

Silence. Emily took a deep breath.

"In fact, I think you should reconsider your relationship with him entirely."

"Aarrgh!" Jericho threw her hands up, disturbing the dusting of snow on her hair. "What is it with you, *Mother?* You didn't like him from the moment you met him. I'm not going to make the same mistakes you made, if that's what you're worried about."

Emily grasped at Jericho in vain as she charged ahead.

"Honey, please. I just don't think that guy is good news. I don't want—" *To see you get hurt.*

"Stop trying to run my life," Jericho hissed, her cheeks blossoming with the cold.

"Jericho, I saw him with another girl. I don't know how serious you are about him, but I don't think he feels the same."

Jericho stopped, a shadow spreading across her face. Emily could read the pain written there. *I know,* it seemed to say. *But I love him.*

More than anything in the world, Emily hated being right. She hated being the bearer of bad news in her daughter's life. Jericho seemed to shut down before her eyes, sheathing the moment of vulnerability within the iron set of her jaw.

"You show up out of nowhere," she spat. "Hang around for a few days, and think you have some say in what I do. It's ridiculous! You don't know who I am. You've never known me."

Tears glistened in her eyes as she poised for the final thrust.

"You don't even know yourself."

She turned and stumbled down an alley, her scarf billowing in the wind.

Emily watched her disappear, a figment in the whirling

white, and squeezed her eyes against the cold. A tremor of sorrow gripped her from within. Would there never be a lasting peace between them? She watched the snow settle on the trash cans and the street, piling white upon the gritty city. *Just like my life. A pristine cloak covering a pauper. A happy smile to hide a gaping hole.* Jericho was right.

"Who am I?" she whispered. Emptiness enveloped her in the silence of the turning snow. She pressed a fist against her chest to ease the pain. "Oh, God," she breathed in the stillness. "Who am I to You?"

There was no answer, only the white and the wind and the cold.

THIRTEEN

EMILY didn't know where she was going, and she didn't care. She had huddled beneath her covers on the sofa, feigning sleep like the coward she was until Jericho had sighed through a bowl of cereal and left for work. Emily had risen then, showered and dressed quietly, called the airline to book a flight home for the day after next, and left. She'd called Ian and Bug with her flight information from her cell phone at a nearby bagel shop, thankful that it was Grant's mellow voice on their machine that greeted her. She wasn't in the mood to fake her way through a cheerful conversation, and breaking down wasn't an option at that point.

So there she was, too apathetic to care where her feet led her, but not apathetic enough to stay at Jericho's. One gritty street followed the next as she wandered. She could only hope she wasn't stumbling into a bad part of town. Emily swore beneath her breath. She wouldn't know a bad part of town if it mugged her and stuffed her in a trash can. They all looked bad to her, and every bum was a pimp or an undercover cop in her imagination. A dark form skittered from the gutter into the street with practiced speed and dove beneath a newspaper. Emily leaped back, skin crawling, and wrapped her arms around herself.

"That's what living in one sheltered place your whole life will do to you," she muttered. "Make you afraid of your own shadow."

How could Jericho stand it? Living alone in such a hostile place? A vision of Jericho's magnetic smile drifted through her mind, and she realized that New York couldn't have been hostile or lonely to her daughter for long. There were too many friends to be made for someone like Jericho, too many adventures to be had, too many men longing for a closer look. Emily shuddered and stopped, rooted to the street by an unpleasant thought. What must it be like to raise a child in such an environment? It had been hard enough in the security and natural confines of a place like Murray. She couldn't imagine it in the heaving, gnashing streets of this city.

A loud noise burst in upon Emily's reverie. She dashed for the sidewalk with burning cheeks as a taxi blared by. What kind of backwoods idiot was she to walk down the middle of the street? She could almost imagine what Grant would say if her were with her, hear his gentle teasing and see Bug's twinkling eyes. What were they up to at home? She realized with sudden sadness that she had missed the Suttons' Labor Day barbecue. There would be others, she supposed, but the thought of her friends and neighbors laughing through bites of Will's burgers and Elsie's potato salad beneath the glow of tiki torches and a thousand autumn stars was almost too much to bear. Bug would have remembered Moscow, of course. The annual badminton tournament wouldn't have been the same without him there to retrieve the wayward shuttlecocks. Had the Hanson twins been up to their usual high jinks? Emily smiled sadly at the memory of Harry gnawing gallantly through the rubber hot dog Robert Hanson had slipped into his bun last year. "Of course I ate it!" Harry had protested later. "I didn't want to offend the cook! It took a mighty pile of relish to work it down, though."

A laugh rang out in the morning air as if in answer to Emily's lonely heart. Happy, childish voices tumbled down the alley to her right. Drawn by the chatter, Emily turned another corner and stopped in surprise. A playground sprawled in cheery colors across the pavement before her, conjured, it seemed, by her own imagination. A group of little girls pushed each other on a row of swings, giggling as they shot up toward the sky. A handful of zealous boys careened after a soccer ball. A sectioned plot of ground in the corner of the yard made a brave attempt at a garden, pushing timid green shoots and carrot tops into the city air.

A hollow *thunk* drew Emily's attention as a little boy booted the soccer ball over the fence to a chorus of groans.

"Why'd you do that, *Chawlie?* Now we gotta go get it."

Emily retrieved the ball from the street and turned to lob it back over the fence. As if by instinct, the children turned as one and skittered inside. She could just throw the ball over and leave, she reasoned, but what if the boys came looking for it? She didn't want them wandering the streets. Compelled by concern and plain curiosity, Emily followed the tall chain-link fence—the only evidence that the little plot of sunshine wasn't in Murray—around to the front of an aging brick bungalow.

"The Hope House, where hearts come home," she read aloud on the sign over the door. What was it? A halfway house? An orphanage of sorts? Something she didn't want to analyze gripped at her heart. Emily knocked on the door. It swung open suddenly, and a boy appeared on the other side. He blinked expectantly at Emily as she floundered.

"Hi. I . . . um . . . have your ball." She held it out as proof. *This is ridiculous.* What was she doing there? The boy nodded curtly, a weird gesture of understanding that made him seem older than he was, and turned away.

"Zanna!" he yelled. "A lady's here."

Emily fumbled for an explanation as a woman materialized behind the boy. A year or two younger than Emily, she was on the tall side, slender, and crowned with a fall of curly dark hair. But it was her eyes that nearly knocked Emily from the porch.

"Jericho," Emily breathed. The same shape, the same set, even the same luminescent color of her daughter's eyes, were there in the stranger's face.

"I'm sorry, can I help you?" the woman asked with the same gray glance from beneath her dark brows that Emily had seen a thousand times. Emily dragged her eyes from the woman's face.

"What is this place?" she blurted, holding out the soccer ball at the same time.

"This is Hope House," the woman said. "It's a home for abandoned children."

Emily nodded, relieved that the sensation that this woman was somehow channeling Jericho was broken with her smile. She was suddenly embarrassed. Undoubtedly, this woman had much more important ways to spend her morning than conversing with a crazy woman.

"I'm sorry. You must think I'm nuts . . . I just wanted to return the ball. The boys kicked it over, and I didn't want them wandering the street looking for it."

There. She had returned the ball. There was no other reason to stay.

"I'm Suzanna Tilberg." The woman stuck out a hand.

"Tilberg!" Emily gasped. *Settle down. It's just a coincidence. A stupid coincidence.* "Is your family here? I mean, I think we might be . . . could we possibly be related? I'm Emily Blyton, but my mother's maiden name was Tilberg. I have to find her . . . and . . . you have my daughter's eyes." Emily's hands flew to her face. "I sound like a lunatic. I'm sorry. It's just that I'm adopted. My birth mother was from New York, and I came here to find my family. I mean, I didn't come here, to Hope House, but I came to New York."

The boy who had opened the door stood staring at her, his mouth agape. When she met his eyes, he quickly closed his mouth and scampered off. She felt her face grow warm.

"I'm sorry," she whispered. "I must be mistaken."

<hr/>

Suzanna relaxed when the woman handed her the ball. Thank the Lord it wasn't Abby's caseworker. Abby was a mess, still crying over the letter her mom had sent her from prison yesterday. It was ten o'clock, and they hadn't been able to coax her out of bed yet. The stranger on the porch was gaping, looking like she was too polite to comment on the horns Suzanna had sprouted. Suzanna smiled and felt herself slipping into showcase mode. It was the danger of living on a shoestring; she never knew when a wealthy benefactor might show up on her doorstep with a wad of cash. There were rumors of such things happening from time to time, and it never hurt to look your best.

This woman didn't seem like a wealthy heiress with a

stricken conscience, however. In fact, she was starting to look more like an escapee from a mental ward somewhere. Suzanna could feel Teddy still pressed against her leg, staring. *I have to get him to stop answering the door.* The woman stuttered through an explanation, and Suzanna felt an odd flutter in her chest as she watched Emily realize where she was and step back into herself. She started to turn away.

Is this it, Lord? Suzanna wondered. *Is this the moment you've been preparing me for? All the pain, all the questions of these abandoned children. Were they leading me to this?*

Suzanna thought about her conversation with Teddy a few days ago. There were so many wounded hearts in the world, most of which she could do nothing about. What a miracle that this woman had found her.

❧

"No," Suzanna lunged for Emily's arm. "No, don't leave. I'm not sure, but I might be able to help."

Emily turned back, torn between hope and despair.

"My mother is Margot Tilberg," Suzanna said. "I think her sister, my aunt, may have given a baby up for adoption. Please." She stepped back. "Come in."

Emily wanted to run. What good would it do her to follow this woman? What could she possibly find? Another dead end? Another family that didn't want her?

"Thank you."

She stepped through the door into the entryway. The house was bigger inside than the outside implied, and although the furnishings were old, the place was tidy and welcoming. To her left was a living room of sorts with a coffee table, couch, and two chairs. A mural graced the wall above the couch, a rainbow and a pair of gentle hands reaching out from the sky. A line of calligraphy ran beneath the hands: "A father to the fatherless, a defender of widows, is God in his holy dwelling."

Emily stiffened. Where had she heard that before? She blushed at the memory of Sunday's encounter with church and the pastor who had reduced her to tears. If there was a God, he seemed to be tailing her. *Great. Just what I need.*

"That's our common area," Suzanna said. "We have up to two dozen kids here at any time . . . mostly orphans and wards of the state, although some of their parents are in prison," Suzanna paused expectantly.

"I'm sorry," Emily said. "You must think this is pretty strange . . . me just showing up on your doorstep."

"You know what's even stranger?" Suzanna smiled. "Somehow I think I knew you were coming."

Emily felt all her bones go soft. She was crumbling, right there in the doorway.

"This is going to sound crazy." There was no turning back. She took a deep breath and plunged in. "I have a daughter here in New York, and she bears a striking resemblance to you. When you opened the door, it was like I was looking into her eyes."

Suzanna nodded. "It would make sense, I suppose. I mean, if we are related."

"How do we find out?"

"Let me call my mother."

⁂

"Jericho?" Emily burst into the small apartment, breathless with excitement. "Honey? Are you here?"

The joy of meeting Suzanna—her cousin, as it turned

out—had buoyed her home. She clutched the address and phone number of her Aunt Margot in her pocket, unwilling to let the paper out of her hand. She had been invited to dinner tomorrow night. Dinner with her real, bone-of-my-bone, flesh-of-my-flesh aunt and cousin. Surely they would be able to answer her questions. Then Emily gasped. What if *they* were there? She allowed her mind to wander through a Hallmark Hall of Fame version of dinner. Her birth parents would cling to her and weep, "My child, my child," while Suzanna smiled and passed the potatoes in the background.

Standing in the entryway, Emily realized she hadn't given a second thought to how Jericho might react to the news. It was as if some divine providence had led Emily to Suzanna that morning, had led her home, really, and as she shot up a halfhearted prayer of thanksgiving in the form of an "it's about time," she decided that nothing could ruin her moment of joy. Jericho would be glad for her, and all would be forgiven.

The dark apartment said otherwise. Jericho usually came home on her lunch breaks, but Emily supposed that was asking too much after the fight they'd had. She couldn't expect the girl to totally abandon her pride for the sake of their relationship. Never mind that Emily had done it a thousand times. She pulled open the shutters and stood alone in the vague gray light. There was a note on the kitchen counter. When had Jericho written that? Was it meant for her? Emily slid her palm beneath the sheet, careful not to crease the paper.

Dear Mom,

I stopped in for an early lunch. Must have just missed you. Or maybe on some level I hoped you wouldn't be here. It's easier for me to say I'm sorry this way. You're right about Mike. I wasn't mad at you last night, I was just mad. I'll try to get off early tonight. I love you.

Jericho

Emily sat on the floor and cried for the better part of an hour. She had her daughter back. The answers to all of her questions and the greatest moment of her life, perhaps, were a day away. Life couldn't get much better. A thousand unsaid thank-yous welled up within her, but who was there to thank? She didn't believe in God, did she? Even if she did, what kind of person would she be to suddenly acknowledge him when things started going her way? She didn't know anything about the Bible, but she was fairly certain God wasn't fond of hypocrites. She had denied and mocked him for the whole of her adult life; now wasn't the time to cozy up to him for a fireside chat.

Emily folded the note carefully and tucked it into her suitcase. She was consistent, if nothing else. If there was an Almighty, surely he appreciated that.

Maybe someday I'll look him up.

FOURTEEN

EMILY willed herself to be still as Suzanna rapped the knocker on the small apartment door. There was still time. She tried to push the thought aside. She could still run if she wanted to, leaving Suzanna and the past behind as she pounded down the hall and yanked open the door to the stairwell.

"This must be Emily."

Emily twitched back to the present and held out her hand.

"Yes," she breathed. "It's a pleasure to meet you."

The older woman—*Aunt Margot,* Emily reminded herself —held her at arm's length.

"Hmmm." She looked Emily up and down. "You're not as tall as either of them, but you have the look of your father in your eyes. Such strange eyes, that one. Always looking, as if he wanted to take in the whole world at once."

Emily dangled between the comments, unsure whether to be flattered or offended.

"Oh, but forgive me. Where are my manners?" Margot's hands fluttered around her apron like loose strings. "Come in, come in. Suzanna, how are you? Did the children like those mittens I sent? I've a pan of pork chops on the stove and a nice bottle of wine in here."

Emily followed Suzanna into the sitting area, absorbing the heavy wood furnishings and crocheted doilies that marked the room.

Margot came back with a bottle of dark red wine and a tray of glasses and began to pour. Emily perched at the edge of a flowered sofa, sensing that she was about to be interviewed.

"So, dear," Margot prompted, "I'm sure you want to know all about your parents."

Emily took her in for the first time, slender and gray and rather nondescript but for the youthful spark in her eyes.

"Yes," Emily said. "All about them. Thank you, Margot."

"Aunt Margot," the older woman corrected.

Emily felt herself go limp, barely able to grasp the stem of the wine glass Margot passed to her. *Please don't let me make a fool of myself.*

"Where do I start?" Margot sat back in her chair, her eyes tracing the line of the ceiling as she searched her memory. "Elizabeth, your mother and my younger sister, was charming when we were young. Not exactly beautiful, but captivating, you know. Even as a child, she could talk her way out of any trouble, only to have it fall on the rest of her siblings." Margot chuckled. "We had some awful rows growing up, but she would always make it up to us, singing and dancing until she coaxed a laugh out of whoever was the maddest. That's just how she was. She couldn't stand to be bored, so she made her own excitement. Of course, our parents worried over her terribly. They tried to keep her in the dark, but she just shone the brighter. I mean, how do you cage a star?"

She smiled wistfully at Emily.

"Sometimes Elizabeth was the worse for it. I want you to know, she was a good person. She had a good heart, even if she didn't exactly think things through. She never meant for things to end up the way they did."

Emily nodded mutely.

"She met your father in the city at a rally of some kind. She went to those sometimes, more for the excitement than to protest anything, I think. He was a handsome college student, and there was an immediate chemistry between them. They were of one mind, you know. Both impatient dreamers."

Margot nodded to herself and paused, drawing out what Emily felt to be an unbearable silence.

"They began seeing each other regularly. Elizabeth didn't keep it a secret, but she didn't exactly broadcast it either. Gerald was poor, while we were wealthy. He wasn't from what society at that time would have considered a good family, and our parents would never have approved."

"Gerald?" Emily asked.

Margot patted her knee.

"Your father, dear. Gerald Montrose."

"Where is he? I mean, could I . . . would he mind if I . . ."

"I'm so sorry, Emily. Gerald is dead. He died in a fire almost twenty years ago."

Something bitter rose at the back of Emily's throat. She had missed her chance.

"I'll never forget the night Elizabeth told us she was pregnant. She was only seventeen. Adoption was the only choice my parents gave her. They hid her away until she gave birth . . . to you."

Margot smiled.

"Almost immediately, there was a couple who wanted you, and the rest is your story to tell."

"You said that Elizabeth *was* charming. Does that mean my mother is dead as well?"

Margot nodded.

"She died of pneumonia several years ago. The stubborn goose wouldn't admit that she was sick until it was too late."

"Did she . . ." Emily paused. "Didn't she ever want to find me?"

"Things were different in those days," Margot said. "She didn't even know the name of the couple who took you, and the city didn't keep the best records back then. But I know you haunted her until the day she died. There was a far-off look she'd get, a sadness that came over her from time to time. I knew she was wondering about you."

Margot roused herself.

"I have some pictures if you'd like to see them."

She disappeared into a room across from the kitchen and came back holding a box with yellowed papers poking out from under the lid. Margot wedged herself between the younger women on the couch.

"I haven't looked at these in years. After Elizabeth died . . . well, in a way, I suppose it was easier to just forget."

She pulled a picture from the box, a small knot of women in the bloom of youth.

"That one," Emily said. "That's my mother, isn't it?"

Margot nodded.

"That's me on her left and your aunt Cecilia on her right. How did you know which one was Elizabeth?"

Emily shook her head.

"My daughter, my Jericho, looks so much like her." She

152

fingered the photograph. "The same eyes . . . the same smile. It's amazing."

Margot hesitated for an instant before laying the picture in Emily's lap.

"Please, take it. I'm sure your daughter would like to see it."

"Thank you," Emily whispered. "I know she would."

An hour later, they were nearing the cardboard bottom of the box. Fading photographs lay scattered across the coffee table in a makeshift collage of the family Emily had never known. A small pile of pictures and crumpled tissues had accumulated in Emily's lap, and though she was overwhelmed by the parade of genetic similarities, there was one face she had yet to see. Cold blossomed in the hollow of her chest as Margot fumbled at the bottom of the box, her arthritic fingers scrabbling for something Emily couldn't see.

"This belonged to Elizabeth."

A hinged locket gleamed on a heavy gold chain.

"This was my mother's?"

"Your father gave it to her. I think there's a picture of him inside. She never took it off, even after he died." Margot suddenly looked sad. "Sometimes I think I should have buried it with her. I'm selfish, I guess, but I wanted something to remind me of her."

"Open it, Emily," Suzanna urged.

Emily rubbed a damp palm down her leg.

"I don't know if I can," she mumbled. Everything had come to this. Every moment of her life, it seemed, had led to this one.

She tugged at the latch. The locket cracked open, and there, suddenly smiling back at her, was her father. She dropped the necklace and jumped up from the couch, heedless of the lock of golden hair that drifted to the floor.

It's him.

Margot and Suzanna rose with her, exchanging worried glances.

"I'm sorry." Emily sank into an armchair. Suzanna retrieved the snippet of hair from her feet and handed it to her. "I'm sorry."

Emily stared at the picture, willing it to speak as she wound the hair around her thumb. He was handsome and so young.

She ran a pale finger over his face, feeling her way to the heart of the matter. Would he have loved her? Would he have held her in his arms or run to her bed when she cried out in the dark of night? Would he have been proud of her? There was no way to know. She swallowed around the lump in her throat.

"You said he died twenty years ago. Didn't he wonder about me too? Didn't he want to know what happened to his daughter?"

Margot sighed. "He didn't know."

Emily felt Suzanna reach over and take her hand.

"He . . . what?"

"He didn't know about you, dear. He never knew that Elizabeth was pregnant. As soon as our parents found out, they sent her away. Once you were born, I was going to tell him, but you were adopted so quickly. I thought it would just cause him pain, knowing he had a child he wouldn't be able to find."

"He didn't know? And now he's *dead?*" That was it. The answer she had been searching for. She was utterly alone in the universe. An accident no one wanted to claim. "But how can I be his child if he didn't know?"

Emily barked out a sob. Suzanna embraced her, and Margot half-rose from the couch, looking uncomfortable.

Emily clutched at her cousin and shook, unable to give the grief a voice.

"I should have told him." Margot's voice trembled, "I'm sorry, I should have told. It just didn't seem right at the time."

"He never loved me. All those times I needed him."

Emily was back in her childhood, trapped in the dark again. Hiding under her bed as her father screamed at her mother in the hall, and somehow she knew that it was all her fault. She covered her head with her hands and whimpered. *I'm sorry, Daddy.*

"All this time," she wept now. "I have no father."

Margot fled to the bedroom for Emily's coat. A shaft of light sifted through the blinds, falling on the small calendar of inspirational thoughts she kept beside her bed. It was too perfect.

She tore off the page and folded it into a square.

Elizabeth would have wanted this.

She tucked the note into the locket and the locket into the inner pocket of Emily's coat.

It's the least I can do.

Suzanna drove Emily home in silence. Emily sat pale and composed in the seat beside her. She had stopped crying abruptly as they left Margot's, preferring to nurse her wounds in private. Suzanna marveled at her control, at the battered shield she pulled over her heart at will, and her dry, haunting gaze. Suzanna, on the other hand, could barely keep her car on the road because of the tears that filled her eyes. She wanted to say something. She wanted to comfort her new cousin and friend, but there was nothing good to be said. She glanced at Emily, noted the set of her jaw, and suspected she wouldn't have heard it anyway.

⚜

They pulled up to the curb in front of Jericho's building. Emily knew she should invite Suzanna in; she was probably dying to meet Jericho.

"Don't worry about me, Em. I know you need to be alone right now."

Emily shifted in her seat. She hadn't expected saying goodbye to be so hard. She reached for Suzanna's hand and gave it a squeeze.

"Thank you." Her voice sounded rusty, an empty bucket hauled from a dry well of grief. "I can't tell you how glad I am that we met." She couldn't say anymore.

"Please keep in touch," Suzanna said. "Call me, write me, whatever you can do."

"I will."

That was it. Emily gave her cousin one last hug and slid from the car, marveling at how easily people slipped in and out of her life. The car pulled away, Suzanna waving frantically as she passed. Emily looked up at the building. She didn't want to go in there, not yet. There was too much in her heart. Too much she couldn't explain, even to herself. She needed some answers, and there was only one place she could think of to look for them.

⚜

Emily hesitated at the door of the church. Why had she come back?

I've nothing left to lose.

The cavernous sanctuary was empty, and Emily wasn't sure whether to feel relieved or disappointed. A choir piped and gloried through practice somewhere else in the building as she walked up the center aisle to the front row. The last rays of the setting sun torched the marvelous stained glass to life, laying a heavy glow across Emily's body, a bar of gold sinking into her self. She felt suddenly small and worthless. There were no answers for her here.

"Can I help you?"

Emily whipped around, embarrassed to be caught in a private moment. It was the pastor, the one who'd greeted her that first Sunday.

"Hello," she stammered. What was his name? Peter? Mark? "Pastor."

He smiled. "Please, call me Paul. It's Emily, right?"

She nodded and moved toward one of the pews. The weight of all that had transpired was suddenly too much to bear. "Tell me something, Paul. Don't you ever wonder about why God does things? I mean, why He allows things to happen to people?"

He sat down beside her. "Sure. All the time."

"Doesn't it bother you?"

"If I could understand everything about God, why He works the way He does and why He allows certain things to happen, He wouldn't be God, would He?"

That was an Ian Mason answer if she'd ever heard one, aggravating because it made sense.

"Why do you think He would let a woman go her whole life feeling unloved? Like she didn't belong?"

"Most people spend their whole lives feeling unloved,

Emily. Even those surrounded by friends and family. On the surface everything is OK, but in those quiet moments when they finally turn off the TV or before they fall asleep at night, they feel helpless and alone."

"Why?"

"Because only the love of God can satisfy us. That's how He designed us, to love Him and be loved by Him. Everything else just falls short."

Emily ran her hands through her hair. This was not what she wanted to hear. "Listen, I just came to New York to find a family I didn't even know I had until recently. To find out who I really am. It just backfired on me, that's all. I'll get over it."

"Emily," he said, "I promise you this. It doesn't matter who you meet or where you look, you'll never find any identity that satisfies you apart from the one God made for you in Jesus Christ."

Her eyes filled unwillingly with tears. "How can you say that?"

"Because there's a hole in your heart that only He can fill. There's a gaping wound that only He can heal. Listen to what God says: 'I have loved you with an everlasting love; I have drawn you with loving-kindness.'"

"Why would God want me?" she whispered. "My own mother didn't. My adoptive father—the one who chose me, for God's sake—regretted it." Emily wrung her hands, forcing the tears back down her throat. "No one has ever loved me with that kind of love. Not even my own daughter." Her voice broke. "My whole life I've been alone. And when I needed God the most, He wasn't there."

"He was there, Emily, but Jesus is a gentleman. He waits to be invited, and I guarantee you something. He'll never force His way into a life where He isn't wanted."

"What are you saying? That God hasn't helped me because I'm not helpless enough? Because I never lay down and died and let the world trample me? Because I stood up for myself when the going got tough?" Emily felt an old pressure building in her, a steaming kettle with no spout. "Christianity is just a crutch, you know."

She couldn't believe she'd said that. She could feel the fires of hell nipping at her sneakers already.

To his credit, Paul didn't answer right away.

"First of all, being helpless enough for God's assistance has never been a problem for anyone, Emily." His eyes grew narrow in the dimming light. "From the moment you drew breath, you were utterly helpless, utterly lost. You've just never wanted to admit it. Secondly, the cross of Christ isn't a crutch. It's a stretcher. We come to Him unable to help ourselves, battered and bruised by the horrors of this world, and sick inside at the secret thoughts we think. We throw ourselves down on His mercy. Only then can He help us."

"But what if He doesn't want me?"

"He does."

"No one has ever wanted me."

"He does."

"But—"

"Emily," Paul said softly, "hasn't He been pursuing you this whole time? Whispering to your heart in that still, small voice that can't be ignored?"

Emily pushed herself up. God haunting her steps as she struggled through life was the last thing she needed. *One more person to disappoint.*

"I'm sorry. I need to get going." She strode to the door, then turned back. "Thank you for listening."

"I'm always here if you want to talk."

She nodded and slipped outside.

⁂

Paul stood at the church door and watched Emily walk away. One more lost soul walking wounded through life, refusing the loving touch of the only one who could heal her.

"God, help her," he whispered. "Please help her."

FIFTEEN

MOM, why would I want to go back home with you? I left there for a reason, you know."

They were sitting in the living room, munching on bagels before Jericho left for work. Emily had come home early last night, too early, from a dinner with long-lost relatives. Jericho hadn't pressed for details at first, but when Emily had calmly said good night and headed for the shower, Jericho had followed.

"What happened?"

"They gave me some lovely photos." She perched on the edge of the toilet, pulling off her shoes and socks.

"That's it?"

"Both of my parents are dead, Jericho. I never knew them, and I never will."

Jericho sank to the edge of the tub.

"I'm so sorry, Mom. I know how much you wanted to—"

"Don't be." Emily gripped her daughter's hands. "I have a

great life." Her eyes shone with a weary intensity. "I have you."

Late that night, Jericho had awoken to what she swore was a muffled wailing coming from the living room. She'd put a pillow over her head and cried for her mother, who would die before she let anyone see how wounded she really was.

A few hours later, they were enjoying a leisurely breakfast together as if nothing had happened.

❈

Emily let her gaze sweep over her daughter's paintings for a moment.

"You say you don't want to go back, but you never really left," she said.

Jericho shifted uncomfortably in her chair, and Emily, sensing that her "fight-or-flight" instinct was about to kick in, scrambled to lighten the mood. "Besides," she said, smiling, "next week is the start of Murray Days. You wouldn't want to miss that."

Jericho groaned and buried her face in her hands at the mention of Murray's annual celebration of everything Western.

"Oh, c'mon. You used to love it, remember? The parades and the mining exhibits."

"I was eight, Mother!"

Emily couldn't help but laugh. "You have to come. You wouldn't want to miss out on a genuine, small-town . . ."

". . . slice of America," Jericho finished, a smile tugging at her lips. "I don't know." She hesitated. "Do they still sell cotton candy out of that cement mixer?"

"It wouldn't be Murray Days if they didn't."

Jericho heaved a long-suffering sigh. "I do have some vacation time saved up at work."

Emily laughed and pulled her daughter into a hug before she could stop herself. "You won't regret it." She winked. "Just think of it as rediscovering your roots. All artists do that at one point or another."

"I know." Jericho rested her head on Emily's shoulder. "I just don't want those roots to become a cage."

Emily caught her breath. *Point taken.* "I know, sweetheart. You're your own woman now. Free to do as you like."

"As long as we're clear on that," Jericho smiled grudgingly. Emily thought her heart might burst. "I'll call the airline and see if we can get the same flight," she said, barely able to keep herself from diving off the bar stool for the phone.

Jericho turned toward the stairs. "I guess I'd better go pack."

⁂

Jericho was surprised at how easy it had been to arrange the details of her life around a week at home. Her boss had gladly given her the time off, saying she needed a break. Her friends had wished her well around mouthfuls of salad on their lunch breaks, then scuttled back to work without missing a beat. Mike hadn't even feigned disappointment at the news of her departure, but pecked her cheek and told her to have fun. She didn't ask him about her mother's accusation. Walking back to her apartment, she told herself it was because she trusted him, but she knew better.

At home, she found Emily folding her laundry for her with immaculate care, a gesture she found both touching and irritating. What would it be like spending a week with her mother at home? Navigating the terrain of their relationship had been hard enough on her own turf, like steering a tank through a minefield. Together they had made progress, but she couldn't shake the feeling that it was only a matter of time until something blew up in their faces.

She squashed their luggage into a taxi the next morning with visions of a relationship doomsday hanging over her. Emily, on the other hand, was almost frantically chipper, filling the ride to the airport with senseless chatter to cover her obviously mounting fear.

"Mom? Mom! You have to settle down. I know you don't like to fly, but at this rate airport security will think you're on speed or something. Just breathe with me, OK? I wish you knew Tai Chi."

When they finally boarded the plane and took off, Jericho offered to hold Emily's hand. Emily declined, but locked the armrest in a death grip that Jericho was sure would snap it off. Several hours and several miniature bottles of Jack Daniels later, they touched down in Denver. Jericho collected their luggage with a woozy Emily in tow and started looking for a cab, when a fluttering hand nabbed her peripheral vision. She dropped her luggage and squealed.

"Bug? What are you doing here?"

"I should ask you the same thing!" Bug laughed and folded Jericho in her arms. "You look beautiful, honey, just radiant. Emily, you didn't tell us she was coming home."

"I didn't know until yesterday," Emily smiled weakly.

"How was the flight?"

"Nauseating."

"Well, you're here now, and that's all that matters. We thought you might be a while, so Ian's parking the car."

Jericho, Bug, and Ian filled the ride home with happy chatter while Emily recovered in the back seat. Mercifully, no one brought up the purpose of her trip. She leaned her head against the cool window and tried to sleep, but her mind seemed bent on reliving every knock-down, drag-out fight she and Jericho had ever had. Memories of screams and tears and cutting remarks pressed in from every side until she felt ready to throw herself from the car. What had she done? She had dreamed of having Jericho home again for so long, but what would become of them now that she was?

I'll find out soon enough.

SIXTEEN

JERICHO cruised the aisles of the drugstore with an arm-
ful of random pharmaceutical products, praying that no one
would see what she had really come for. Several happy days
had passed since she'd arrived home with her mother, and
things were going surprisingly well. Emily worked in the garage
while Jericho painted or slept in. They took Moscow for long
walks in the woods and barbecued with Ian and Bug and Grant,
and by some minor miracle they didn't fight. Jericho had been
enjoying herself and feeling truly relaxed for the first time in a
long time, until an innocent glance at the calendar over Emily's
sink had nearly paralyzed her. *A week, only a week overdue.*
Still, it was unusual. After twenty minutes of trying to convince
herself that her lateness was just because of the stress of the last
few weeks, Jericho dragged herself to the store.

    She hesitated as she made her way toward the registers. How
many of the checkers knew her mom? Wasn't there some sort of

cashiers' code of ethics that kept them from talking about what they saw? She made a beeline for a teenage girl manning the express lane. Hopefully she wouldn't ask questions.

"Jericho!"

She whirled around with a stifled shriek and clutched the boxes against her chest. Grant Mason was headed her way. She glanced down, and to her horror saw the pink box poking out between the Tylenol and the toothpaste. Surely he wouldn't know what it was. He had never gotten a girl into that kind of trouble.

"What are you doing here?" she asked breathlessly as she shifted her bundle.

"Just picking up a few things. You know, deodorant, gum, that kind of stuff. You?"

"Same." Oh, no. He had slipped into line behind her. How was she going to distract him while the cashier rang up her stuff?

"Ma'am? I can help you next."

Jericho piled her things on the conveyor belt with two twenties and turned to face Grant. "So . . ." she scrambled for a topic. What did he like to talk about? Sports? Current events? "Tell me about God."

"What?"

"Tell me about God. You know a lot about God, right?"

"I wouldn't say I know a lot."

Jericho felt the blood fleeing from her brain. What was that cashier doing? Calling for a price check on her pregnancy test?

"Just tell me!"

Grant gave her a sideways look.

"OK, what would you like to know?"

"Why does He always send tornados to trailer parks?" *Are*

you out of your mind? "I mean, how do we know that He's even a 'he'? What if God's a woman?"

"Well, the Bible always refers to God with male references like 'he' or 'Father,' but since God is Spirit, He's really neither male nor female."

The checkout girl was holding out Jericho's change and her bag of purchases expectantly.

"Oh. Thank you. That makes a lot of sense, Grant. Hey, I've got to go, but I'll see you later." She grabbed her things and jogged for the exit. Outside, she felt a hysterical titter rising in her throat. She had lost it, totally and completely. Taking that test was the last thing in the world she wanted to do, but if she didn't, the suspense would undoubtedly drive her over the brink of sanity.

Later, she sat huddled on her bathroom counter at home, losing sight of herself as steam billowed around the mirror. She clutched the little white stick in her hand, afraid to look at the business end. The instructions had been easy, but she'd read them twice anyway and found a new mantra along the way. *Pink means pregnant. Pink means pregnant.*

A knock sounded on the door. Jericho jumped up, dropping the stick at the sound of Emily's voice.

"Honey? I'm going to run into town. Do you want anything from the store?"

"No, thank you," she answered quickly, almost running over Emily's words. "I'm just going to jump in the shower." There was a moment's pause.

"OK. I was thinking about making burritos for dinner. Sound good?"

"Yes. That sounds great."

Jericho turned off the water and waited until she heard the Bronco grind down the driveway and into the street before she turned around. There it was, nestled in the fluffy nap of the bath mat. How strange that a three-inch snippet of plastic had the power to forever alter her life. She nudged the mat with her toe until the strip clattered onto the bare floor.

Pink.

⚜

"There was never anyone else. You know that."

"Do I?" Mike's voice was tight, defensive and unfeeling.

"You said you loved me." She hated how desperate she sounded, like just another simpering female.

"I did, in my own way, but things change. I mean, I was *responsible*." He hung heavy on the word, as though it were his claim to nobility. "I made sure we used protection. I don't know how this happened, but it's not really my—"

"Problem. It's not your problem, is that it?"

"I was going to say issue. Listen, I do care about you. I'll send you some money for . . . whatever. You're a smart girl, you'll be OK. Look, I've gotta go. Let me know how things work out."

There was a click on the other end, then silence. After a minute the receiver began to pulse a warning in Jericho's ear, but she couldn't put it down. She couldn't even move. How had she been so easily dismissed? He was her boyfriend. He'd said he loved her. And now she was, what? An inconvenience?

"Forgotten," she whispered as she lowered the phone. "Abandoned."

He's just like Dad. I'll never be good enough.

The tears were unexpected, seeping out from a wound she had plastered over long ago. She crawled onto her bed and pulled the familiar blanket over her face, seeking comfort but finding none. She was on her own again. *Just like old times.*

SEVENTEEN

"OOOH!" A chorus of croons rose as Song pulled a pair of tiny socks from a pile of colored tissue.

"These are precious," she sighed. "Thank you so much. I can't wait to get this child out of me and into these." She rubbed her swollen belly with a grimace.

"Don't worry," Elsie soothed, patting Song's knee. "Your time will come. Someday, this will all be a memory."

Song smiled. "Soon. Make it come soon."

Emily's living room was a sea of pastel streamers and balloons. Mounds of tissue frothed around Song's ankles as she opened one present after another at the impromptu baby shower.

"Where's Bug?" she asked as she pulled at the ribbon of another gift. "I thought for sure she would be here."

"She couldn't make it." Emily called from the kitchen, where she was working on a tray of sandwiches. She was glad Song couldn't read the lie in her face. "Something came up at church."

In truth, Emily hadn't invited her. Bug, in her compassion, hadn't asked yet what Emily had discovered in New York, but Emily knew she would, eventually. Emily felt herself grow heavy at the thought of that moment, when her closest friend would see just how worthless everyone else thought she was. She would do whatever she could to delay that moment, even lie.

Selma hovered around Song like a satellite, snapping pictures, to the younger woman's dismay.

"Please," she protested. "The fewer pictures of me in this state, the better. I went to the community center last week for that maternity swim class I told you about." She grimaced. "I swear the instructor almost called animal control. She thought she had a stranded whale on her hands."

A chorus of moans and soothing clucks rose from the other ladies.

"Nooo. You look great."

"You're glowing."

Song snorted, a note of desperation caught between laughter and tears. "That's because I'm generating enough heat to cook dinner for all of you."

Emily chuckled from the kitchen and sliced more sandwiches into dainty triangles.

꧁

Jericho pulled a sheet of tiny quiches from the oven, willing her hands not to shake. What should've been a joyous occasion was a nightmare for her—a vision of her own future, she feared, filled with rancid diapers and sippy cups and her mother's endless drone of advice blaring above some Barney video.

"Jer?" Emily laid a hand on her arm. "Are you OK?"

Jericho went cold. The pan of quiches quivered over the sink as she groped for something to say.

"Why is it," she forced a shaky laugh, "that mothers get so nostalgic around pregnant women? I, for one, feel for Song. The rest of you seem to take some kind of strange pleasure in her misery."

"No, that's not it at all. We just remember what the experience was like," Emily said. "We know about all the joys and trials that await her. Hopefully more joys than trials," she added as an afterthought.

Out in the living room, Helena laid a bulging card on Song's lap. "Open this one next."

"What is this?" Song tore at the envelope. Squares of paper fluttered to her lap. "'This coupon entitles the bearer to one free hour of babysitting,'" she read. "But there are dozens of them!"

"I told a few of my friends about the shower," Helena explained. "They wanted to get in on the action, so we decided to give you something truly practical," she grinned. "Don't worry—these girls are super-responsible, with lists of references a mile long. They've babysat for practically everyone in town at one time or another."

"I'm sorry." Song snuffled into a fistful of Kleenex. "I just get so emotional these days. Thank you." She squeezed Helena's hand, crumpling a handful of coupons in the process. "This is a wonderful gift."

Emily headed into the living room carrying a tray of sandwiches and a bowl of fruit.

"Eat up, ladies. Especially you, Song. You need your strength."

Behind her, Jericho tottered between the countertops. A

cold damp rose on her neck as her stomach climbed toward her mouth and the reality of being a single mother washed over her. There was only one thing to do, she thought as she wove toward the bathroom. Only one thing to do.

EIGHTEEN

SHE couldn't believe how easy it had been. Just a matter of picking up the phone, and even that had been easier than she'd expected. Even after she'd baldly blurted out her request—it sounded so bad when she actually said it—the soothing voice on the other end had assured her that everything would be all right, that she was doing the right thing.

Jericho scrounged through her purse for the bus fare and quietly thanked the driver as she climbed aboard. Denver and her appointment were only two hours away. The shuttle lurched into motion as she found a seat, and as she pinched at the pressure points in her neck that, according to what she hoped was a reputable website, were supposed to quell nausea, she wondered if taking the bus was a wise choice after all. What other choice did she have? There was no one else in Murray she could have begged a ride from, not without arousing enough suspicion to bring the Spanish Inquisition down on her head in the form of her mother. With the right excuse, she could have borrowed the old Bronco and driven herself, but Janine, her crooning counselor at the clinic, had said she wouldn't be able to drive after the procedure.

Jericho shifted uneasily in her seat. It wasn't the physical discomfort connected to this option that worried her; it was all the euphemisms surrounding it. Why were they trying so hard to make this seem like a pleasant thing? It was an awful thing she was about to do. Tears leaped into her eyes. She turned to the window. But it just wasn't meant to be. She could hardly take care of herself, let alone someone else.

The bus slowed for a stoplight. A baby swathed in pink lifted a plump arm to pat her mother's face on the sidewalk outside. The little girl radiated delight as she buried her face in the woman's neck, and suddenly Jericho couldn't breathe. *It isn't fair.* She was an animal caught in the jaws of a cruel trap, and there was really only one thing to do.

The light changed. The bus lurched forward and left the happy family behind. Jericho fumbled in her bag for her CD player and slipped the earphones over her head. There would be plenty of time to think about things later. Right now was the time for action. She turned up the volume, desperate to lose herself in the song, but running beneath the music was a low refrain. It sounded like an infant's cry.

❧

Helena busied herself about the shop. She had gladly volunteered to watch the store that morning so that Song could get some rest, but now she wasn't so sure. She just didn't feel right. It wasn't really a physical sensation, but a nameless, growing dread that darkened over her like a cloud. She dusted

176

Emily's display pieces in the window and rearranged the shelves of herbal remedy books at the back of the store to keep her hands, and hopefully her thoughts, busy. Twenty minutes later, she still couldn't decide whether to order the books alphabetically by author or by herb.

"Lavender . . . majoram . . . mint . . ." she mumbled as she sorted the tomes. A figure materialized in her peripheral vision. Helena gasped and the books slipped from her hands.

"Helena . . ." Grant hurried across the room and crouched to help her pick up the books. "Sorry. I shouldn't have snuck up on you like that. I'll wear a bell next time."

Helena laughed. As their hands brushed together over the books, she felt the fog around her start to lift.

"I'm sorry." Her hair bounced over her shoulders as she shook her head. "I don't know what my problem is today. I've just got this feeling. I know it sounds bizarre, but it's like there's a storm brooding. Like something bad is headed this way."

"Maybe it's a sort of intuition," Grant offered. "Like how the rabbits at Harry's place always flip out before it snows."

She gave him a playful shove. "Oh, lovely. I'm a rabbit now, am I?"

"Well, I could've used any number of examples." He smiled, "Stinkbugs in mating season get really crazy."

"G-r-a-a-n-t!"

Laughing, he hauled himself up shelf by shelf and offered her a hand. "So what is it? What's bothering you?"

They made their way to the front of the store. Helena stopped at the window and let the sun spill over her face as she closed her eyes.

"I don't know," she said. "It's nothing, really. I feel better already just talking to you."

"Well," he said, his voice sounding almost tender as he reached for her hand, "I'm glad I could help."

"No!" she whispered fiercely.

⁂

Grant dropped Helena's hand like a hot rock.

"Sorry," he muttered before he noticed that she was staring intently out the window. Was there an animal on Main Street again? Elk were common enough, but maybe there was a bear.

"No," she whispered again.

He followed her gaze to a shiny car purring up to the curb. It was an old Corvette, immaculately kept, the kind that owners buffed nightly with a jealous fervor. The door swung open and a man stepped out, tall and handsome in a manicured sort of way. He turned, out of habit it seemed, to admire the car's gleaming curves before surveying the town.

Helena blanched with an almost palpable nausea, and Grant didn't know whether to steady her or step out of the way.

"What is it?" he wondered why they were whispering.

"It's my father." she breathed, her lip lifting in an unconscious curl. "He's here."

⁂

The bus shuddered and groaned to a halt at the station. Jericho climbed off and found herself feeling very alone. The clinic was an easy walk from here, she reminded herself, and Janine was waiting. *Janine.* The woman assigned to Jericho as her counselor had made it abundantly clear from the very beginning that this was Jericho's decision, no one else's. Why then did she feel so pressured into doing this? Why did she feel like she would be letting Janine and a whole clinic of kindly doctors down if she didn't show up? Why had this, the most drastic of options, suddenly seemed like the only one?

"Why did I agree to this?" she mumbled as she passed through a crosswalk.

The clinic was ahead on her left: a clean and cheery place with a group of women huddled on the sidewalk outside. She made her way up the steps and through the front door.

"Hi," she whispered to the receptionist, then found her voice. "I have a one o'clock appointment."

"And which counselor set this up for you?" the woman asked. Very calm. Very professional.

"Janine."

The receptionist pecked at the computer. "If you'll just have a seat, someone will be with you in a moment."

Jericho nodded and drifted into the waiting room, clutching her bag. There were pamphlets everywhere. Safe sex, AIDS, pregnancy, condoms.

"I should have come here before I met Mike," she mumbled, but somehow she knew it wouldn't have helped.

"Jericho?"

That was Janine walking toward her. The bespectacled young blond could have been no other.

"Welcome. It's such a pleasure to finally meet you."

Jericho shook the offered hand and found her fingers squeezed in an icy clutch.

It's just my imagination. I'm sure she's very nice.

Janine adjusted her trendy glasses, the frames unnecessarily thick for her pretty face, and Jericho wondered what the woman was trying to prove . . . or hide.

What's wrong with me? She's a professional.

"If you'll just follow me this direction, we can get started."

Jericho felt herself gaping as they passed through a hallway. Happy families and babies smiled at her from the walls.

"We're not anti-family, Jericho," Janine said, smiling at Jericho's reaction. "We just know that sometimes these things happen when we're not ready. Timing is everything in life. But I'm sure you already know that."

Janine propped a hand beneath Jericho's elbow and steered her around a corner. The irony of the situation was almost unbearable. They looked like friends meeting for lunch or heading off to their favorite bar for happy hour, not recent acquaintances about to—

A high-pitched giggle escaped Jericho's lips. She fought for control.

"Jericho?" Janine's face hovered near hers, a picture of professional concern.

"I, uh . . ." The room was so close, so sterile.

She could smell cleaning solvents mingling in the air and wondered what the fumes were doing to her baby—and in that moment she knew. She was about to rid herself of this problem. What did she care what chemicals she breathed?

Kill my baby. I'm about to kill my baby.

"Please," she gasped. "Restroom."

❦

Twenty minutes and two lunges for the toilet later, Jericho's knees solidified. She blotted her temples with a damp paper towel as she leaned against the stainless steel sink. Janine had already stopped in twice to check on her, but the effort was too little, too late. Jericho had seen in one terrible moment of incongruity the absolute horror of what she had planned to

180

do. There was a baby growing inside her. All the euphemisms in the world couldn't change that.

Bile welled up in her esophagus, and she ran back into the nearest stall, thinking as she retched that life and death wavered so easily in this place. She wasn't going to kill her unformed, innocent child, no matter what Janine said.

NINETEEN

HELENA ran a brush through her hair and grabbed a jacket. Grant would be there any minute. She still didn't understand why he had insisted on picking her up instead of just meeting her at the dance.

"Men," she murmured. "I'll never understand them."

She could only hope that she would be able to enjoy the evening, that it would take her mind off of her father's unexpected arrival. He had come to see her, he explained during their one brief and very civil conversation. He said he missed her.

The sound of urgent honking interrupted her thoughts. Grant waited at the curb behind the wheel of a chuffing jalopy. He leaned across the seat and flung open the passenger door as she hesitated on the sidewalk.

"Your chariot awaits!" he yelled over the chug of the motor. "I'm sorry I didn't come to the door. I'm afraid to get out. This thing doesn't have a parking brake, and if I turn it off, I may not be able to start it again!"

Helena slid in beside him, heaving the door shut behind her. "How are we going to get home after the dance if this thing won't start?"

Grant's mouth fell open, and she stifled a smile at his chagrin. "Um . . . a romantic walk beneath the stars?" he sighed. "I'm sorry. I know this thing is a piece of junk. I didn't want you to have to walk into town. I wanted to take you there in style."

Helena clamped her lips together and closed her eyes. She wouldn't laugh . . . she couldn't. Who knew how deeply his ego was tied to this humming lump of rust?

"In style?" she squeaked.

"Well, you know, I thought we might have a shot at making the society pages of the *Denver Post*." He shot her a wicked grin.

She giggled and yanked at her seatbelt.

"Careful now," he warned as he eased away from the curb. "Wouldn't want to scratch the Naugahyde."

Helena rolled open the window and leaned her forehead against the frame, relishing the fingers of the summer darkness in her hair. What was it about Grant that put her so at ease? They'd shared the intimacy of old friends, from the very start it seemed. She felt his eyes on her and smiled.

"Shouldn't you be watching the road?" she asked.

He dragged his gaze back to the winding road. Trees brushed at the night sky, softening the horizon and painting stars into the darkness. A mountain breeze filled the car, and Helena felt as though she had never drawn a breath before that moment. She closed her eyes and let the mountains fill her senses. Then she felt it. Her cool hand being tugged out of her lap, wrapped in Grant's warm palm. She opened her eyes. He smiled and stroked the back of her hand with his thumb. *Old friends, huh?*

⁂

Jericho sidled over to the makeshift bar and ordered a drink. If one more wannabe cowboy called her "purty," she'd throw up on his boots. She thanked the bartender, who looked suspiciously like her mother's dentist beneath his ten-gallon hat, tucked the lemonade discreetly in the crook of her arm, and found a seat on a stack of hay bales in the corner of the long hall. The barn social was one of the highlights of Murray Days every year, and she could remember begging her mother to let her go as a little girl.

"Be careful what you wish for," she muttered.

Those days seemed like memories from another lifetime. She watched a father twirl his little girl around the dance floor, scattering hay as they went. Things had been so much simpler when she was young. Now, she was going to be a mother. Even stranger, her trip to the clinic yesterday had confirmed in her mind that she already was one.

Speaking of mothers . . . Emily seemed to be having the time of her life, swinging from one dance partner to the next. She linked arms with Harry, and he turned her gently around the floor, telling her something that made her throw her head back and laugh. Neighbors circled around them, clapping and stomping in the hay as the fiddles whined.

Jericho shook her head. It was amazing, the life her mother had made for herself in Murray. Friends who were more like family surrounded her. She had a thriving business and a place carved out for herself in this mountain community.

No wonder she loves it so much. Then a thought assailed Jericho. Why hadn't she ever seen this side of her mother before? Was Emily this happy only when her cantankerous daughter wasn't around? Or had she always been that way?

"Maybe I was just too self-absorbed to notice," she whispered into her cup. Memories filled her mind: Emily taking food to sick neighbors, hosting wedding showers in their cramped living room, helping at every car wash, blood drive, and charity auction the town held. "She has a home here because she made a home here." Jericho sighed. "I don't seem to belong anywhere, but I suppose that's my own fault."

A shadow fell across her lap. She squinted up into the flashing lights above the dance floor.

"Can I help you?" she asked, inwardly cursing herself for sounding like a rude New Yorker.

The bale creaked with the weight of someone sitting down beside her. She set her cup down and shaded her eyes. He was older, but handsome in the polished way she was used to seeing in the city.

"Would you like to dance?" he asked, never taking his eyes from her face.

"Well, I'm not really—"

"I know," he soothed. "This isn't really my thing either. I feel like I've stepped onto the set of *Hee Haw*." He smirked. "But everyone seems to be having a good time." He grabbed her hand and dragged her toward the dance floor.

Jericho stumbled after him.

"I'm not sure—"

"Oh, c'mon," he said smoothly. "You look like you could use a little fun. When in Rome." He pulled her into the throng and held her against him as the music slowed. Jericho allowed herself to be maneuvered around the floor while she considered her options. She could drop-kick him . . . a knee in the groin was always effective . . . an uppercut right under his chin might work. She stopped herself mid-thought. For pete's sake, he wasn't a mugger, just an overzealous suitor who'd had one too many. She sighed. She supposed she could endure one dance with the guy, just to save her mother the embarrassment of a scene.

"What's your name, sweetheart?" he asked.

"Jericho." She gritted her teeth and smiled.

"Mine's Jim. Jim Jantzen."

Jantzen. Jericho felt her smile drop as Helena's face flashed through her mind.

"No." She pushed against his chest. "I can't dance with you."

"Why? What's going on?" He stepped back, but still gripped her hand. "I thought we were having a good time."

"No!" Jericho wrenched her hand free. "You're not someone I want to dance with, OK? Let's leave it at that."

Jim backed off.

"Aren't we touchy?" He laughed and clawed at the air, "Me-ow." He laughed harder at his own joke. "Get it? Haw haw haw . . . because you're catty . . . haw haw."

Jericho felt her eyes narrow as the foul words flew from her lips, and felt a stab of guilt at the humiliation she was undoubtedly causing her mother.

⁂

Helena smiled into Grant's neck as they danced. There was a faint, woodsy scent to him that she loved, as if he lived perpetually in the open air. Not like the gigolos who used to pursue her at the beach, tan and shiny, with their silk shirts

187

unbuttoned just enough to reveal their hairy chests. She giggled at the thought of them hiking through the woods, the trees clawing at their hair and their cologne attracting bears.

"What are you doing to my neck down there?" Grant laughed. "It tickles."

Helena sighed. "Sorry. I was just thinking about what my life used to be like in Miami."

"Do you miss it?" He brushed a strand of hair from her cheek.

"Not at all. That's the weird thing. I mean, there are friends that I miss, of course, but my life was so different." She shook her head. "It's almost like I was a different person. I cared about the stupidest things." She pulled back until their eyes met. "There's something about this place. It's so simple. Everyone knows what's really important. There just seems to be a clarity about life. I can't explain it."

"It's the lack of oxygen." Grant laughed as she pummeled him.

"Let go of me!" A sudden screech from across the barn stilled the crowd.

"What's going on?" Helena whispered.

Grant craned his neck.

"I don't know. Probably someone had too much to drink."

"Come on, baby. Why are you so feisty?" a voice said, chuckling.

Helena went cold.

"Oh, no," she whispered. "Please, Dad, not here."

She dropped Grant's hand and hurried through the crowd, propelled by a sick curiosity. Maybe she could stop him; maybe she could distract him somehow before things got out of hand.

Too late.

Jim Jantzen was hunched over a bale of hay, supporting himself with one hand and clutching his stomach with the other. Angry tears glittered in Jericho's eyes. She flapped a hand as if to shake off the sting of the punch.

"That's a spicy girl, that one," Jim grunted.

Jericho turned and stalked away. Helena pushed her way closer.

"I can't believe you," she hissed. "How could you come here? We left Miami to get away from you, you know."

Jim straightened and reached for her.

"Honey—"

"Don't touch me! You make me sick. I am so ashamed of you."

She wormed through the crowd toward the exit. Grant met her at the door.

"Please," she whispered, "just leave me alone."

TWENTY

EMILY rose the next morning feeling stiff and sore. Too much dancing last night, she thought as she slogged through a bowl of bran. Too much beer. And yet there was something else beneath it all, a deep rheumatism of the soul she refused to dwell on. It had been that way since she came back from New York, like a splinter trying to fester to the surface of her heart. She tidied the kitchen and looked for something else to do. Jericho hadn't surfaced from her room yet, and although Emily desperately wanted to talk to her daughter, she knew it would have to seem natural. She couldn't just stand there like the breakfast nazi waiting for her daughter to wake up. She grabbed Moscow's brush from a drawer and went to town on his haunches, much to his groaning delight. Half an hour and a wastebasket full of fur later, Jericho was still asleep. Moscow frolicked around the room, looking ten pounds lighter.

"OK, boy, I give up. Let's go work in the garage."

Several hours later, Emily's growling stomach demanded that she take a break. She met with the sound of running water as she slipped in the back door. At least Jericho was up and showering; it was a start. Lunch would necessitate a trip to town, she realized as she rummaged through empty cupboards. She wasn't really in the mood for a drawn-out trip to the store, but the deli wasn't far away. She could pick up a pastrami on rye for Jericho. Not an authentic New York pastrami on rye, but still a thoughtful gesture.

The small deli was packed with the usual lunch crowd of locals and tourists. Emily grabbed a number ticket and slipped into an empty booth near the counter, relishing the smell of fresh potato salad and dill pickles and the bustle of the butchers behind the counter. The bell over the door jangled as Helena squeezed through. Emily called her name before she realized that the girl might just want to be alone. Last night hadn't been exactly pleasant for her. Helena grabbed a ticket and slid into Emily's booth with a smile. Apparently, she was choosing to ignore her father's indelicate behavior.

"Doesn't this place have the best honey-baked ham?" Helena said. "I was never a fan of the stuff until I moved here. Now I can't seem to get enough."

Emily relaxed. There was no pretense about Helena; she was like a breath of crisp mountain air in an otherwise stifling room.

"Did you and Grant enjoy yourselves last night? I can imagine Murray Days is quite a hoot, especially for an outsider."

"Yeah, we did, for the most part." Helena's mouth hinted at a grimace, but she quickly drew herself up again with a smile. "He's such a great guy. I really appreciate his friendship."

"Not bad-looking, either," Emily said slyly.

"No." Helena twirled a straw airily. "He's actually quite handsome, if I say so myself."

They were giggling together like twelve-year-olds when the door jangled open again. Emily's heart sank as Jim Jantzen walked in. But Helena's back was to the door, and there were a lot of people in there. Maybe she wouldn't see him.

"Jim Jantzen." His voice was unmistakable. It looked to Emily like he was fawning over the petite blond beside him in line.

Helena stopped laughing. Emily grabbed her hand.

"Let's get out of here," she whispered. "Forget about him, OK? We'll go for a walk."

"No," Helena said slowly, rising from her seat. "I need to talk to him."

⚜

If Jim was startled by his daughter's sudden appearance, it was only for a moment. He turned away from his new friend and focused his full attention on Helena.

"Honey, what a nice surprise. It's not every day I get to have lunch with my best girl."

She dodged the arm he tried to drape across her.

"What are you doing here?" she hissed.

Jim put on a face of wide-eyed innocence.

"I'm hungry. I hear they make a mean egg-salad—"

"That's not what I mean, and you know it. I can't believe you came here. Don't you know what this is going to do to Mom? Haven't you hurt her enough?"

The hum of the busy deli fell silent as customers stopped to watch the unfolding drama.

"I didn't come here to see your mother," he whispered,

obviously hoping Helena would follow his example. "I came here to see you. I came to see my daughter, because she's almost eighteen and halfway across the country and out of my life."

His polished features sagged, his perfect white teeth suddenly seeming out of place in his desperate face.

"What do you want from me?" Helena asked. "I hope it's not forgiveness, because I don't think I can give that right now."

"Listen, I know you hate me." His eyes suddenly shifted, staring past her into a bleak place. "But I don't want you to carry that kind of bitterness around your whole life. I don't want you to think that all men . . ." A hand flopped in resignation. "Are like me."

Helena felt at the booth behind her and sat down beside Emily, never taking her eyes from her father's face.

"I don't hate you." Her gaze shifted to the door. "You need to leave now."

"Please, baby—"

Helena made it to the door in two steps and left the screen swinging behind her.

⌘

Jim pulled on his sunglasses and made to follow Helena.

"Let her go."

Emily checked herself. What was she doing? Cozying up to the philandering Floridian would bring gossip to her door faster than Moscow brought squirrels, but he looked so lost, like a little boy watching his house burn to the ground, and she knew with a piercing clarity what he was feeling.

Jim was looking at her.

"I think she just needs some time alone."

Silence.

"That's how it usually works after my daughter has stormed out of the room," she finished lamely.

He flopped down across from her in the booth and groaned into his palms, "What have I done?"

Emily opened her mouth to remind him, then shut it quickly. He was a smooth amalgamation of every man who had ever hurt her. Even so, her snide comments wouldn't help.

"Well," he said when she didn't answer, "seeing as you seem to have some experience in the area of domestic bliss, why don't you tell me your name, and then perhaps you can give me some more advice."

Emily studied her thumbs. He was brutally handsome, and at a second glance she thought perhaps he resented his looks. What had they ever brought him but trouble? She couldn't help but wonder what his father had looked like. And was he kind?

"What is it?" Jim's brow creased.

"I'm sorry?"

"You're staring at me. Is there something wrong?"

"Oh." She blushed and dipped her head. "No. Of course not. I'm Emily . . . Blyton."

He shook the offered hand, and she squirmed, as only a handsome man sizing her up could make her do.

"You look vaguely familiar."

"That was my daughter you were hitting on at the dance," she blurted, unable to resist.

"Ohhh." His eyes were suddenly veiled and cool. "Well, my apologies."

"No," Emily backpedaled, "please accept mine. I'm sorry she laid into you like that. Jericho, well . . . she's been in New York for a while."

"It was my fault." His hands found one another and nested. "I don't know what I was thinking."

"You weren't."

Jim grimaced. "Are you always so abrupt?"

"I don't know any other way to be," she said. "Besides, your relationship with your only child is at stake here. Do you really want to waste time on pleasantries?"

"What can I do?"

It was a rhetorical question, but Emily couldn't sit still.

"You apologize. You start acting like the father you should have been all along, and you wait."

He leaned across the table, his eyes keen on her face. Emily felt the edge of a flush, but refused to give in.

"Why," he asked, "is this so important to you?"

"I have a daughter. I am a daughter." She couldn't meet his eyes. She wanted to laugh and curse at the sudden bulb in her throat that signaled the onset of tears. "I've disappointed so many."

He dropped his own hand and reached for hers. It was hardly a romantic gesture, more like one soldier fortifying another in the trenches, but Emily glanced around, aghast.

"We do the best we can," he whispered fiercely.

With that he disappeared, closing the door quietly behind him, and Emily was left with her wayward thoughts and a tear bobbing in her lower lashes.

⚜

"I'm home."

Emily breezed through the screen door, stopping to feed a tidbit of roast beef to Moscow as she set their sandwiches on the counter. He pressed against her leg, lifting his nose at the delicate scent of Swiss cheese.

"Hello?"

An afghan lay wadded on the couch. The television flickered mutely, a game show contestant springing around the set at the prospect of winning a new car. Emily took the stairs two at a time with the pastrami in her hand, but stopped on the landing at a familiar sound: a muffled sobbing coming from Jericho's room.

Emily groaned softly. She knew it. That East Coast loser had broken her baby's heart. Better sooner than later, she supposed. She knocked softly on Jericho's door.

"Sweetie?"

The sobs stopped abruptly. Emily heard tissues being pulled from a box and Jericho straightening the covers on her bed.

"Honey, I won't bother you if you don't want me to," Emily said to the door. "I just want you to know that whatever it is, I'm here for you."

The door opened. Jericho stood in her pajamas, tears leaking down her lowered face. She looked so small. Emily pulled her into an embrace.

"I'm sorry, baby. Whatever it is, I'm so sorry."

"Oh, Mom," Jericho cried, pressing a fistful of tissues against Emily's back, "you don't know the half of it."

"Then tell me. It can't be that bad."

Jericho barked a short, bitter laugh and retreated back to her bed.

"Mike and I broke up."

Emily nodded.

"It's *why* we broke up."

"Tell me. It's OK."

Jericho looked down at her hands. "I'm so ashamed," she whispered. "Mom, I . . . I'm pregnant."

Emily almost laughed at the irony. All her fierce attempts to protect Jericho had just driven her onto the same path she herself had taken. *What a twisted world.*

"I was so careful." Jericho shook her head. "I swore to myself that I'd never make the same mistake you did. I promised myself that I'd never end up like you. No offense."

"None taken." Emily crept to Jericho's side and smoothed the hair from her face. She had a feeling that this moment and how she handled it would determine much of their future together. "I'm sorry, honey. This is my fault. All those years . . . if I'd just been different. If I'd just shown you how much I loved you, you wouldn't have gone looking for affection somewhere else."

"What are you babbling about, Mom? I didn't get pregnant because of some emotional wound you inflicted on me. I really liked Mike, and I really liked sleeping with him. This is my own stupid fault." She picked at the edge of the comforter with a vengeance.

"But why did you sleep with him?" Emily pressed, then blushed at the look Jericho shot her. "OK, besides the obvious. What was it you liked so much about being with him?"

"Mom!" Jericho wailed. "I'm an adult. I don't have to sit here discussing this with you."

"I think you do."

"Fine. Aside from the obvious," she rolled her eyes, and Emily caught a glimpse of the pouting teenager grown into an adult. "I liked the way I felt with him. He made me feel really special." Her voice fell to a whisper, "This is ridiculous. I need to figure out what I'm going to do."

"It's not ridiculous. I'm trying to apologize here. I'm sorry

I wasn't . . ." What was the use, anyway? "I'm sorry I wasn't the mom I should have been," Emily finished lamely. "Maybe you wouldn't have ended up here if I had been." No response. "What do you think you'll do, anyway? Do you . . . want an abortion?" Emily cringed. *Not my first grandchild.*

Jericho shook her head.

"No. I already tried that. I couldn't do it. I wouldn't be here today if you had done that to me." She straightened her shoulders. "This child will have a shot at life. A pathetic, emotionally malnourished, joke-of-a-mother shot at life, but a shot nonetheless."

Emily scooped her daughter into her arms, feeling her stiffen for a moment before she relaxed.

"I'm scared."

"I know," Emily soothed. "But you'll be OK. I promise, you'll be fine."

TWENTY-ONE

EMILY stomped toward town. Grass crunched beneath her boots, and she shivered despite the baking afternoon heat. Would it never rain again? The whole world was desperate and dry beyond relief, and part of herself responded to its agony.

She didn't know where she was going, but after rocking a distraught Jericho to sleep, she had to get out of the house. There was too much anger roiling in her gut to stay still, and the last thing she wanted was to upset Jericho with her foul mood.

What was it with men? Were they somehow genetically wired to desert their offspring? Maybe that's why her dad had been so miserable and mean all the time. He was fighting nature.

"Young Miss Blyton, where are you off to at such a pace?" It was Harry, waving his cane at her from his deck. "Stop and sit for a spell. All that tearing around is what keeps you from putting any meat on those bones."

Emily turned and charged up the hill with hardly a pause. Maybe Harry could help her sort things out. There was a lot of wisdom beneath those tangled brows.

"Oh, dear." Harry shook his head at her as she neared the house. "What on earth has gotten into you this time?"

She took a moment to catch her breath as he ushered her inside for their usual cup of tea.

"You look a mite upset, Emily." He stumped around the table to join her. "Has something happened?"

"Yes," Emily sighed. "No. I don't know. I just don't know how it always comes to this."

"What is it?"

"Harry, are there any good fathers in the world? I mean good, loving ones who actually stick around?"

Harry hesitated, as though unsure of whether she really wanted an answer.

"Yes. There are many good fathers in the world. I know you're still upset that he didn't tell you the truth sooner, but your father was a good—"

"No, he wasn't!" Emily jumped up, banging her chair back against the counter. "He wasn't a good man, Harry. He hit me sometimes. Did you know that? He never had a kind word for me, and nothing I did was ever good enough. That was my father. That was the good man everyone talks about." Her throat was raw with bitterness. "He didn't love me. Even at the end, when he lay dying. He couldn't say the words."

"I'm so sorry, Em." There was genuine sorrow in Harry's features, like a line of careful knitting pulled apart. "I didn't know. If I had known he'd laid a hand on you . . ."

"It's OK," she murmured. "It's OK, Harry. That was a long time ago."

"And look how well you've done despite that," he said. "You have a wonderful life and a wonderful daughter. You've taken something bad and brought good from it. That shows a lot of character, and that's something you've given Jericho too."

"You know what I've given my daughter? Promiscuity, and apparently fertility. Some legacy."

She walked to the window over the sink and leaned her ribs into the counter, staring despondently into the afternoon as tears pressed forward from behind her eyes.

"What are you telling me?" Harry leaned over his tea. "Jericho's pregnant?"

Emily thrust her hands into her hair, stomped her foot, and cursed herself loudly, then burst into tears.

"Hang on, now," Harry limped from his chair and circled her as though she were a skittish horse. "It's OK."

"It wasn't my secret to tell," she sobbed. "My daughter can't even trust me."

"Emily." He reached for her hand and gently untangled it from her hair. "You're working yourself into a fit. You've got to settle down. I won't tell anyone about Jericho. You know I won't."

"It doesn't matter. Everyone will know soon enough."

"Does she know who the father is?"

"He doesn't want anything to do with her or this child. He said he didn't love her like that. Maybe men don't love their children like women do . . ." She hung her head. "Maybe they just don't have the capacity for that kind of love."

"Emily!" Harry growled suddenly. "Enough of this."

She sank back into her chair. Had she ever seen Harry angry before?

"I won't listen to you running us down anymore. I know you've been hurt, and you have every right to be angry, but there are good men in the world. There are good fathers." His voice fell to a gravelly whisper. "I was a good father."

"Harry?"

"You don't know what it's like to lose a child." He mopped a wayward tear from his cheek. "What it's like to lose a son."

"I didn't know. I thought Gloria couldn't . . ."

"At first it seemed like we wouldn't be able to have children. There was something about Gloria that made it hard for her. We went to the doctor a couple of times, but back then there wasn't much you could do, just keep trying. Finally, God blessed us with a beautiful little boy. Matthew. My little Matty. Imagine how thrilled we were. He just lit up our world, such a smart little fellow. Life was grand, even in the hard times, because we were a family."

"What happened?"

His eyes trailed up toward the ceiling. "He was four years old when he disappeared. Those were the worst few days of my life, when we couldn't find him. The whole county was here looking, combing the hills for any sign of him." His eyes met hers again, milky with grief. "Three days later, they found him at the bottom of a well." Harry tapped his neck. "He broke . . . he broke his little neck. I loved my son, but there was nothing I could do."

"Oh, Harry," Emily moaned. "I had no idea."

He shook his head. "We didn't talk about it much. It just hurt too bad. Darn near killed Gloria. We didn't try to have any more after that." He sighed again. "I'm surprised your parents never mentioned it."

"Well," Emily stared at her hands, "we never talked enough. Not about important things."

"I know. Your parents—your parents here in Murray—were far from perfect, but they loved you. I know you're feeling kind of adrift right now," he went on as she opened her mouth, "what with not knowing your real father and feeling like you didn't know your dad here, either, but don't let it destroy what you've got, Em. Don't let it ruin who you are."

"That's just it," she protested, "I don't know who I am."

"I think you do. You just don't want to see. Sometimes we look long enough at ourselves, and we realize we don't like what's there."

"What are you saying, that I'm a bad person?"

"No. I just think you don't want to admit . . . I mean, you've got a lot of wounds that you haven't been able to heal. I don't think you want to accept that you need something more than what you can provide."

"I'm not sure what you're talking about, Harry. But hey, I . . . uh . . . have to get going. Thanks for listening, I feel better already," she lied. "I'm so sorry about Matthew," she added in a low voice as she opened the door. "But thank you for telling me."

Emily practically ran into town, eager to leave the overwhelming sorrow and discomfort of Harry's house behind. He was a kind old soul, but she was trying to move on with her life, not wallow in the past.

The mingled smells of lavender and incense drifted through the open door of Song's shop on a breeze that stirred the wind chimes hanging over the sidewalk. Emily slipped inside.

"Song? Helena?"

Song waddled out of the back room with a sandwich in her hand. She was tucking a crumpled envelope into her pocket.

"Hi, Emily. Come sit down. Have a snack with me."

"Actually, I just came to see if you have anything for nausea. I . . . Jericho has a touch of the flu." She hated lying to

Song, who would undoubtedly sympathize with her daughter's predicament, but what else could she do?

"The poor girl. I have just the thing." Song handed her a bottle. "It's ginger tea."

"Thank you."

"What's wrong, Emily? You seem a little sad."

Was it that obvious?

"I don't know. Do you ever feel like everything's wrong with the world, and there's no one to make it right? Like you're totally on your own?"

Song nodded. "At least once every day." She pulled the envelope from her pocket and handed it to Emily.

"I sent that to Ling last week. It's a picture from my latest ultrasound. I wasn't trying to entice him back or anything, I just thought he might want to see his son." Her voice dropped. "He sent it back. He didn't even open it. I know how you feel, Emily, because I feel like that almost all the time."

Emily pulled her friend into a hug.

"No crying, now." Song patted Emily's back. "Can't let the customers see you upset. It's not exactly an endorsement for my natural antidepressants. There's a case of St. John's Wort back there that I've been trying to move for months. C'mon, help me stock some of this new inventory. It'll take your mind off things. Besides, I can't bend over anymore."

⁂

How Emily ended up at the Masons' that night, she couldn't have said. She had just called Jericho to tell her she was coming home with dinner, and the next thing she knew, she was eating cookies in Bug's kitchen, hoping for an answer to a question she couldn't even articulate. She felt like a ship whose rudder had snapped off in a storm. There was nothing for her to do but be battered on the rocks.

Emily helped Bug dry the dishes before she drifted into Ian's study. There was a Bible open on his desk and a faraway look in his eyes.

"Ian? Why am I so miserable?"

She couldn't believe she had just spoken those words. Why had she opened her mouth?

"What?"

"I don't know, I just feel so awful. Like when you get a paper cut and it bleeds forever. Death by paper cut, can you imagine? Never mind, I'm just rambling."

"There's a giant, gaping wound in you, Emily," he said. "You're miserable because you're just starting to realize that you can't heal it yourself."

"Sure I can." She wandered around the small room, looking at Ian's pictures: Ian digging a well somewhere in Africa, Ian playing soccer with children in Mexico. "I've always done everything for myself."

"By choice."

"What?" *Of all the insensitive things to say.* "Was it my choice that my mother got knocked up when she was seventeen and gave me away to strangers without ever telling my father she was pregnant? Was it my choice that my adoptive father didn't want me? That he was always ashamed of me? Was that my choice, Ian? Was it my choice when Rick left me with no money and a daughter to raise?"

"Many people have abandoned you in your life. No one's denying that, Emily, but I'm not talking about people. There's One who won't abandon you. One who can heal all your hurts, who has been pursuing you with perfect love since the day you were born." He hesitated. "You've turned your back on

God more times than I can count. That's why you've had to go it alone."

"Oh, give it up, Ian! I appreciate the nice thought, but you've got to stop pushing God on me. Geez, you're like a dog with a new bone."

"Sorry. You're the one who asked." He swiveled his chair back toward the desk.

What was this? A bit of temper in Ian Mason? He was always the one nagging her, wasn't he?

"Fine," Emily clipped. "I'll explain this to you nice and simple. I am not interested in *God* because *God* has never been there for me. I've been through some tough stuff, and there's no evidence that He was ever hanging around to help. Maybe I'm the exception to your little rule, but God never showed up to help me."

"He's been there all along, Em. Waiting for you to let Him in."

Jesus is a gentleman. Paul's words echoed in her mind.

"God abandoned me!" she hissed. "He left me for dead every chance he got."

Ian crossed the room and put a gentle hand on her shoulder. "Emily, he didn't abandon you. That's the farthest thing from the truth—"

Emily shoved his hand away. "Then where was he when I was eighteen and pregnant and terrified? Where was he when we had to move back in with . . . my father?" She choked on a sob. "Where was he when I was trying to raise a child on my own?"

"Emily . . ."

"No! God has never been my father. He was never there when I needed Him. Where was he," she sobbed, "when my own daddy wouldn't love me?" Ian reached for her. She stumbled away. "When my flesh and blood threw me away, hoping someone else would find the scraps? And where was he when my adopted father—the one who chose me, for God's sake, the one who was supposed to love me—pushed me away? When the only time he touched me was to smack me for some childish mistake?" She sank into Ian's chair and sobbed into the crook of her arm. "I don't need another father, heavenly or otherwise."

Ian stood at a loss for words.

Bug, hearing the commotion, appeared at the door. "Honey, I'm so sorry." She pulled Emily into an embrace.

"No." Emily shoved her away. "I'm sorry. Please." A vice clamped onto her heart. "Just leave me alone."

She stumbled out the door and fled into the night.

TWENTY-TWO

IAN rocked slowly on the deck behind his house, his hammock swayed by a warm breeze. A plate of half-eaten sandwiches rested on his chest, and a glass of lemonade sat sweating on the deck beside him. His lunch break should have been quick. He had too much to do to be lounging in the sun, but Bug had insisted he lay down for a minute. The minute had become an hour, and still he couldn't move. It had been one of those weeks, the kind that made him want to grab Bug and hightail it to Tahiti without looking back.

There had been an awkward and ill-advised wedding for two desperately lonely people who collectively had already suffered through four divorces. Some people never listened. Some people never learned. Then there was Travis, the seventeen-year-old wunderkind, who, despite Ian's attempts at counseling, was driving his parents mad. Somehow it was Ian's fault that Travis had been pulled over on his way to

Denver with a joint pursed between his lips. Never mind their seventeen years of neglect and undisciplined living. The church needed new everything, and the budget still wasn't balanced . . . and then there was Emily. Just thinking about her kicked Ian's heartburn into high gear. He offered her daily, almost hourly, into God's hands, but it didn't make watching her self-destruct any easier.

Ian groaned and rolled over. He was expected at the Nelsons' fiftieth anniversary party that night, and the last thing he needed was a body covered with waffle marks. Sometimes he couldn't help but wonder: Why did life have to be so hard?

The fire refines.

Oh, great. His mind was parroting back the Sunday school answers he'd heard since childhood.

Your faith is more precious than gold.

Ian groaned again as he sat up. It had been a rhetorical question. He hadn't really been looking for an answer. Geez, wasn't he allowed to be cranky once in awhile?

Clouds had gathered in the distance, teasing the mountains again with the empty threat of afternoon rain, and on the breeze Ian caught a whiff of something disturbingly familiar. Who was stupid enough to attempt a campfire in these conditions? You'd have to be brain-dead not to know about the burn restrictions the state was under, and every trailhead had giant signs announcing the ban on fire of any kind. Even tourists would see those.

Ian scanned the horizon, shading his eyes against the sun. The belly of that cloud bank was so dark. A puff of sickly black smoke trailed into the sky from the forest near Emily's cabin, followed quickly by two more. That wasn't a campfire . . .

"Oh, God, help!" Ian leaped up and ran for his bike. "Bug!"

he hollered. "Call the fire department. Call Tim. There's a fire near Emily's!"

He plunged down the hill on his bike, shooting up a silent prayer for protection as he wrenched his front tire from one boulder to the next. He'd be no good to anyone if he broke his neck on the way there. Ian tried not to think about the terrible fire that had consumed several towns in the southern part of the state last year, burning a dozen poor souls alive as they'd tried to flee. It had been faster and more ruthless than anyone could have imagined.

What if Emily was working in the garage? What if Jericho was napping upstairs? The flames would be on them before they knew it, gobbling at the timbers of the house, and not a drop of water in sight to save them. His teeth clapped together as he hit the bridge, shooting pain into his neck, but he kept pedaling with all the strength his burning calves possessed. The air was already growing thick and dirty, every breath tinged with the sour taste of burning wood. Ian lowered his head, spitting flecks of ash from his mouth. In the distance he heard the muffled groan of trees wrenching open in the flames. It was coming.

He tossed the bike onto the porch and ran into the house.

"Emily!" Silence. "Jericho!"

He ran back outside. Sweat poured down his back, drying quickly in the rising heat. He stumbled, coughing, toward the garage.

"Emily!"

She met him halfway up the driveway, grease smudged across her wrists and her cheek, a look of sheer terror on her face. "Ian!" She doubled over, coughing. "What's going on?"

"Forest fire," he shouted over the growl of crackling brush. "Over the hill. It's coming this way."

She dropped what looked like a fuel pump. "Ian! My house! What am I—"

He grabbed her arms and shook her. "Where's Jericho?"

"She's in town. She took Moscow to the groomer's."

"Get the Bronco. We've got to get out of here."

Emily turned pale. "I can't."

"What do you—"

"I can't! It wouldn't start this morning. I was trying to fix it. I just took out half the parts."

Ian went limp. He couldn't breathe, he couldn't move, and soon he would burn down to little more than a pile of carbon. *The fire refines. So this is how I'm going to die.*

Emily grabbed his arm and dragged him away from the garage.

"C'mon, Ian, we have to run."

"We'll never outrun it."

"We have to try," she wailed. "I don't want to die!"

The desperation in her voice shook him from his stupor.

"This way."

They wove through the trees, dizzy from the billowing smoke. Ian glanced back and saw flames cresting the hill behind them like the yawning mouth of a vast furnace.

"Oh, dear God, help us!" he choked. "Move, Emily! Move!"

"I can't see! It's too dark."

Indeed, the belching breath of the inferno had blotted out the sun, plunging them into an unnatural twilight. Ian's lungs burned as he pushed her on.

"Get down," he barked. "Run low to the ground, or this smoke'll kill us."

❧

Emily doubled over and ran as fast as she could. Already, her skin was burning in the searing heat. She heard a crack and an earth-wrenching groan behind them. *My house.*

She thought of the pictures in her closet. If only she had put them in the album Elsie had given her, she could have dashed into the house and grabbed them. Instead, the fire was devouring them, licking apart the snapshots of Jericho's first birthday, her first steps, her first dance at school. Why was this happening?

God is punishing you. Getting you back for what you said. He's just like every other father you've known.

Here was the proof, rolling from the jaws of hell through the tops of the trees and the underbrush, but there would be no satisfaction in telling Ian that she had been right all along.

A deer thundered past them in the dark, a flaming branch caught in his antlers.

Emily began to cry, the acrid smoke stinging in her chest.

I don't want to die.

Ian let out a muffled yelp. Ahead of them, the smoke began to clear.

"I think we can make it!" he yelled. "We're almost—"

And then he disappeared. Emily fumbled in the empty darkness.

"Ian? Where—" Her foot caught on a rock. She tripped and tumbled face-first toward the ground, but the ground wasn't there. She fell for a second or two in stunned silence before the air shot out of her with a grunt as she hit uneven earth.

She rolled onto her side, cursing every muscle in her body. Ian moaned not far from her. They had fallen into some kind of pit. A ravine, at least ten feet across and equally as deep. She dragged herself to her feet and limped over to where he lay.

"Ian? Are you alive?"

"Regretfully," he said, clutching at his calf. "I don't need to see it to know that I won't be going anywhere, anytime soon." Emily pulled gingerly at his pant leg, drawing it up toward his knee. His boot and sock were soaked in blood, and his foot lay wrenched at an unnatural angle. A splintered, white bone protruded from his skin. She bit her lip. It was not the time to panic.

"Yeah, I think mountain biking is out of the picture for a while." She drew a deep breath. The air in the crevice was fresh, barely tinged by smoke. "I think the fire turned the other way."

"Let's clear out all this brush," Ian grunted. "Anything flammable."

They still had time, she told herself. Someone would find them. Emily scrambled through the thickets, pulling out the thorny clumps by their roots and flinging them over the edge. Thorns dug into her cuticles. She willed her trembling hands to stop. She wouldn't allow herself to be scared.

Ian was a sickly shade of gray by the time she returned. She pulled off her jacket and rolled it into a pillow as she eased him down onto the rocks.

"I think I broke a few ribs too." He groaned.

"You may not be able to preach for a few weeks, but I think you'll be fine." She forced a cheerful note into her voice, "This'll make for a great story. 'Yea, though I walk through the valley of the shadow of death,' and all that." She lay down beside him, fitting her back against the rocks. "We'll be okay. You'll see."

Even as she spoke, a cloud slunk down into the ravine, and as she gasped for a breath, she wondered if it was death she tasted in the air.

The fire leaped the ridge high above them in an effortless bound, orange smoke devouring the breathable air. Pinecones popped in the roar of the marching flames, and limbs groaned as they tore from their trunks. Emily clutched her streaming eyes, covering her mouth with the crook of her arm.

"Oh, God!" she sputtered. "Ian—"

"Stay low," he ordered. "Stay in the ravine. We'll be OK."

"But there's so much brush down here. The fire could—"

"You'll be OK."

"How do you know?" she gasped.

"Fear not." He closed his eyes. "For I have redeemed you; I have summoned you by name; you are mine."

The pain was causing him to hallucinate, she thought, a merciful turn of fate. Maybe he wouldn't remember any of it.

"When you walk through the fire, you will not be burned; the flames will not set you ablaze."

"What are you talking about?" Her lips burned with the taste of carbon. Ash settled on them like a sickly, gray snow.

"It's Scripture, Em." Soot caked in the creases of Ian's face as he forced a weak smile. "'I am with you always, to the very end of the age.' God will never desert His children."

"Oh, Ian," she cried, tears drying in her eyes before they could fall. "I'm not His child. I'm no one's child." She yanked at Ian's shirt as his mouth fell open and his head lolled onto her arm. "Ian? Ian!" He lay unconscious for a moment, then jerked forward, his eyes rolling open again.

"Emily." He sunk his fingers into her arm. "I've seen it, Em. The fire. It's coming. It's almost here." Coughs racked his frame. "You've got to go," he croaked.

She shook her head. "We'll be OK. You said so."

"Emily." His eyes gleamed with a strange new light as he looked past her. "Run. Run, Emily, run!"

"No!" she sobbed, choking on a flurry of ash. The roar of the flames was deafening. "I won't leave you."

In a swift and seamless motion, he rolled to his knees, hooked her beneath an arm and a leg, and flung her up over the craggy lip of the ravine. She scrambled for a handhold.

"Run!" he barked. "Run! Run! Run!"

She clawed her way to her feet, blind in the smoke and the violating heat. The forest sizzled around her, trees roaring into flame as the beast leaped from one to another. The fire bore down on her.

"Ian!" she screamed, crouching over the ravine.

"Run," she heard him gasp. "Run. Oh, Jesus, Jesus." She turned and grappled up the rocky slope. Heat seared her legs as she stumbled blindly in the darkness.

"Help me," she gasped. Her throat squeezed shut. "I can't breathe." She felt herself falling, bashing into a rock. Voices called from a distance. "Jesus!" she sobbed. "Jesus!" Darkness settled over her, and a horrible, searing pain. "Jesus . . . Daddy! Daddy!"

TWENTY-THREE

LIGHTS penetrated the fog, bright and blurry, a consuming world of white. And pain. Fire. Emily moaned at the rustling around her ears. It was close. *God help us. Ian. Ian.* Voices murmured in the distance.

"I think she's coming to."

She drew a painful breath and screamed. *Help! Help us!*

"She's moaning."

"What's she trying to say?"

The light grew brighter, pressing in on her, burning her eyes.

"No." Emily moaned and thrashed in the back of the ambulance.

"Do you think we should restrain her?"

"What, are you crazy?"

"I don't want her to hurt herself."

"We're almost to the hospital."

"C'mon, Em. Hold still. Just a little longer."

Emily opened soot-lashed eyes to find three worried fire-fighters huddled over her.

"Wh-hat . . ." Flames leaped in her chest and her throat.

"Shhh. Don't talk, Emily."

Was that Tim? The eyes beneath the layers of ash looked familiar. She lifted an arm and gasped at the sudden wash of pain. What happened? She felt like a rag doll carelessly tossed into the wash. Where were her ribs? Were they even connected to her body anymore? And what was that grinding weight on her chest? Where was Ian? She turned her head with effort. Where was his gurney?

"Try not to talk, Em. You've suffered some smoke inhalation." She rasped again.

"What's that?"

"I–Ian . . ." she wheezed. "Ian."

There was a moment of heavy silence, a quiet sob from the corner, and a hissed admonition to shut up.

"Emily." Tim knelt beside the gurney and took her hand. "Ian is alive."

"Where?"

"They took him in the helicopter."

She didn't have to ask.

"He was burned, Em. Badly. They needed to get him to the hospital quickly."

Emily felt a fiery pain in her gut. She had just enough energy to roll onto her side and vomit before the lights went out.

⁂

The hospital was a fog of waking and sleeping, light and dark, punctuated by the awful smell of burning. Doctors poked and prodded her, pumped oxygen into her lungs and shone lights into her eyes, and finally released her after a night of observation.

She limped over to the burn unit the next morning. Grant was keeping watch outside his father's room with the air of one thrust forever into shadow, never to see the sun again. She closed her eyes and screamed at herself not to cry.

"I need to see him," she whispered after giving Grant a motherly hug.

He shook his head.

"I don't know if now is the time, Em. You're still weak yourself. It might upset him. He needs to rest."

Grant was obviously scrabbling for any excuse. Emily set her jaw and dodged around him.

"No!" he yelped and leaped for the door.

"Grant."

They froze in the dim hallway, eyes wide.

"Let her in," Ian moaned from inside the room.

Emily expelled the breath she had been holding. Grant opened the door.

The hospital room was like any other, she realized upon later reflection, the nondescript sterile floors and furnishings, the walls and curtains in soothing pastels. It was the seeping mass of gauze groaning in the bed that made her ankles fold.

"Oh, God!" she croaked. "How could this happen, Ian? How could he let this happen to you?"

"It's not as bad as it looks."

Was he laughing at her? A bandage fluttered near his mouth. What kind of drugs were they giving him?

Emily dragged herself into a chair near the bed.

"Stop crying."

"I can't. Ian, your poor hands . . . your legs. How will you . . ."

"Listen. I'm alive." He paused for a ragged breath. "So are you. We shouldn't be."

Emily gripped the side rail. "I should be the one lying in this bed."

"You shouldn't be here at all."

"What do you mean?"

Ian's face twisted as he raised his head. His eyes burned through the drug-induced clouds with the clarity of pain.

"God showed up for you. I saw Him, Em. I saw Him in the fire. He spread His arms out over you. God saved you from that fire because He loves you."

"I don't believe you."

Ian cried out as he lifted his arms.

Emily jumped from the chair.

"Then there is no proof," he growled, "that will be enough for you."

She fled the room.

TWENTY-FOUR

TIMOTHY Vilfroy sighed as he sifted his boots through the wasteland of wet ash west of Runner's Creek. There was something intrinsically sad about the scene, a subtle light and breath missing from the place that wouldn't return for many years. Even the fragrant breeze that had once stirred the fields of columbine was still, and its absence left a deeper wound somehow than any of the other, more blatant horrors he had seen over the years.

After two years of training at one of the country's most prestigious fire schools, twelve years of hosing down the charred remains of warehouses and subsidized housing as a firefighter in Philadelphia, and nine years of service as the fire chief in Murray, he had seen his share of devastation, but never so close to home. His own home, lovingly built for his family by his own hands, lay a scant four miles to the east, a hiccup for such a fire.

"Like the wrath of hell itself."

As head of the department it was his job to file the official report. It was his job to determine what had caused the blaze.

Lightning.

It was lightning, of course. Everyone had seen it striking the mountain that day. Why, then, was he bashing around through this tinderbox looking for an answer? Logs crumbled beneath his boots as he climbed the hill. The few charred trees that remained at the crown flung their blackened limbs toward the sky like lepers begging for a healing touch. A high, dirty haze refused to vacate the area, casting a sickly glow and dredging up the still-frame shots of horror that his mind refused to delete.

He skirted a blackened boulder and remembered. There was the little girl in his second year as a firefighter, the little girl with the frightened eyes and the long, dark braids, screaming for him to save her as he'd shimmied around the ledge of the torched apartment building. She'd leaped toward his arms a fraction of a second too soon and had fallen like a stone two stories to the pavement, where she'd shattered nearly every bone in her tiny body, but somehow managed to survive.

He'd visited her in the hospital later, propelled by an unhealthy guilt, only to be wept over and kissed by her mother as if he were some kind of savior, and all the while the little dark eyes had probed him from behind the bandaged face. He'd made it into the hall before he retched into his hands.

And there was the jumper in his twelfth year, the year that had driven him from the city to the peace of this mountain hamlet. The young man wavering on the window ledge had pulled one pill after another out of his dirty pocket and sent them sailing toward the earth. No one had really thought he planned to follow, except for his pretty, pregnant wife, who'd run back and forth in the street below, chasing after the pills and shrieking that he needed to take his medication. Tim had grabbed the young man from an open window and hauled him back toward the safety of the building, blinded by adrenaline, unable to see the knife the jumper pulled until it was too late. The blade had plunged deep into Tim's side, narrowly missing his lung, and in that instant Tim had flinched, and the bird had sailed away.

Several days later, outside the firehouse, the pretty, pregnant wife had thrown herself at him, screaming that he'd killed her husband, that her child was fatherless because of him. He'd never forgotten her face.

Then there was this time Tim had plunged into the throat of the dragon itself, really afraid for the first time in his career, blind and mute and half-deaf from the creature's roar, led only by a feeble mew for help. He had tripped over Ian Mason and almost discarded him for a broiled stump, the time he had pulled Ian, blistered and senseless, from the flames.

Shuffling alone through the dead forest as he sorted out his life's most painful moments, Tim found tears surprisingly near the surface. He stuffed his fist into his mouth to muffle the quiet sobs.

Ian, the best man he knew, the one who had talked Tim and Sheila down from the ledge of a bitter divorce just two years ago, who had helped Tim to carry his grief when his younger brother was killed, who understood his pain and his mistakes and never judged. Ian was a mummy now, bound like the forest to a long period of pain.

And Emily—sweet, strong Emily Blyton—braving hell to stay by Ian's side. Tim hadn't been the one to pull her out, but he imagined that she had fared much the same. He would miss her pretty face and the smooth skin on her lean, tanned arms.

Tim ground the heels of his hands into his eyes and cursed. *Enough.* What was done was done. He had a report to finish. He pressed on toward the wide ravine where he had found Ian, toward the burning slope the others had plucked Emily from. He wasn't usually one to fault the Almighty—it had been more years than he could remember since he had braved even the back row of a church—but sometimes he couldn't help but question the justice of it all.

He hauled himself over the lip and out of the ravine, dumbstruck that a battered and broken Ian had mustered the strength to throw a grown woman over it. Anything was possible with enough adrenaline, he supposed.

His boots fell on something soft, a distinct change from the grit and crunch of dead earth. He glanced down and froze. Gooseflesh rippled up his spine to the back of his neck and over his arms. The forest was silent, suspended in a wayward shaft of light, and he felt it coming: a cool, fragrant breeze caressed the land. He sank to his knees.

"Oh, holy God," he whispered.

❧

"I'm not sure how to tell you this, Emily." Tim paced the length of his kitchen, cracking his knuckles as he cradled the phone with his neck. He almost hadn't believed the news that Emily had escaped from the fire unscathed . . . almost. He realized that Emily was waiting for him to say something, and in a moment of panic, he lost his power of speech. Tim squeezed the fingers of his left hand, popping through each knuckle in a rapid fire.

"Tim, please stop cracking your hands. Just say whatever you need to say."

He grabbed the phone with his right hand and shook out the left one sheepishly.

"You should be dead, Emily," he blurted, aghast at how bald that sounded. He was the fire chief, for pity's sake. "What I mean is, you shouldn't have made it out of there alive, and I don't know why you did."

Emily snorted. "I guess I got lucky. Some luck, huh?"

"No, you don't understand. Listen, I don't know what to put in my report because I can't explain this. It goes against all the laws of physics and fire that I know. Fire just doesn't behave that way. Emily," he pleaded, "I should be attending your memorial service today, not talking to you on the phone. Thank God I'm not, but you have to trust me on this. I need you to come with me. Please, I need you to see this."

"And what will I see if I come?"

"Apparently, Someone wanted you to stick around for a while."

❦

An hour later, Emily slogged through a wasteland of sodden ash at Tim's side. She knew that this had once been the wooded area behind her house, but even so she could hardly believe it.

"I used to bring Jericho here for picnics," she murmured as she wrenched her borrowed firehouse boots from a pile of mud. The earth seemed to be sliding away from beneath her, the blackened soil itself fleeing the scene of destruction. "How were you able to put this out so fast? I thought these things usually raged for weeks."

"They can." He nodded, helping her over a charred boulder. "But conditions were in our favor this time. The drop in temperature, the lack of wind, even that little bit of rain helped. Amazing that the lightning that started this was part of the storm that helped put it out. Plus, we got the call early. If Ian hadn't—"

Tim stopped, suddenly aware that Emily was turning the color of aspen bark. He grabbed her arm and propelled her forward.

"Let's, uh, let's skirt the plateau here and continue south. We're almost there."

Very diplomatic, Emily thought, but she didn't resist him. She had no desire to see the charred remains of what had once been her home. She and Jericho had been living at the hospital and at the Masons' for the past week, unwilling to think about what the future held. Thank goodness she had insurance, but it didn't make her feel much better.

Tim was waiting for her. She trudged on blindly behind him, trying to block the horrific scenery from taking root in her memory. Why had he dragged her out here, anyway? Was this some twisted attempt at therapy? Confront your fears and be healed? She had a feeling her cheery yellow boot would end up in his backside if that was his plan.

"Here. It's over here."

Emily stiffened at the unfamiliar tremor in Tim's voice. What could be awful enough to make burly Tim Vilfroy cry? She picked her way down the hill until she reached his side.

He was standing in some sort of ditch, and Emily realized with an electric jolt that it was the ravine where she and Ian had almost died, every crevice of it charred black with soot. She could still smell the smoke, and in the distance she could hear the roar of death marching over the trees.

She let out a strangled cry and staggered toward the far side of the ravine.

"Get me out! Get me out! Why did you bring me here?" she sobbed as she clawed at the unyielding rock. She gained a foothold and clambered for the edge.

"Emily, wait!" Tim barked. "Get down. You're going to hurt yourself."

She caught the protruding lip that had kept Ian from escaping and hauled herself over it with a strength fueled by sheer panic, only to collapse weeping on the other side. Tim scrambled up the slope behind her, taking significantly longer to clear the rim. She was on her knees, her face pressed to the earth and her hands in front of her, like an ancient nun working through some invisible rosary.

"Emily," Tim whispered. "Look."

She noticed the feeling of something cool and soft and slick beneath her wrists. Rock and shattered pinecones gouged her legs, but her arms lay cradled on a pillow of fresh . . . *grass*. Emily opened her eyes.

She knew it. She had actually died in the fire, and due to some administrative error, she was being allowed one glimpse of heaven. There was a clump of perfect columbines and a slender aspen tree stretching toward the sky in an oval of untouched grass. The horror lay around her, rolling its black tongue over the land, but there, in that small sanctuary, all was safe.

"What is this?" she gasped.

"It's a miracle."

Emily began to shake.

"This is where we found you, Em."

God showed up for you.

But it couldn't be.

No evidence will be enough for you.

A glint of something golden caught her eye. Emily trembled

to her knees. There, caught in the branches of the aspen, hung Margot's locket. The heavy hinge, so tight before, fell open in her hand.

A father to the fatherless . . .

She choked as tears closed her throat.

. . . is God in his holy dwelling.

How many times had Emily run to her favorite perch over the town in search of solitude, of comfort, of answers? But the comfort had always been momentary. The answers had never really come. And she'd never left there feeling any better. Now, she ran her thumb over the locket and waited in the immense silence of the trees. Would God speak to her?

"I'm listening," she whispered, "if there's something You want to say."

Isn't there something you want to say?

"I'm . . . sorry, God. I'm sorry for blaming You. I'm sorry for saying You were never there." Tears rolled down her face, leaving starbursts on the rock beneath her. "I know now that You were there all along." She lifted her face to the trees. "I'm wounded, God. I'm not a good person."

Let Me heal you.

"Ian says that You sent Your Son to free me from that stuff. That He died for me and took all the pain of my mistakes so I wouldn't have to bear it. I believe it. I can't help but believe it." She began to weep. "Oh, God, I'm tired of carrying this around. I'm tired of running from You. Please take this pain away and make me whole."

Emily Blyton curled on her side and wept, warmed by the sun and the strange, new light in her heart.

TWENTY-FIVE

ALMOST two weeks had passed since the fire, and Jim Jantzen was starting to feel a slight glimmer of hope. He had spent the last several days being useful, cleaning soot and ash from the sidewalks and storefronts on Main Street, helping the town get back on its feet. He had even driven Song Tao to the hospital in his Corvette when her water broke right in front of him and she went into labor two weeks early. He was being selfless and helpful. He was starting to feel like a man again.

And so he decided, with great reluctance, to go home. Helena wasn't going to forgive him anytime soon, and although he was growing attached to this charming town, he knew his presence was only making life difficult for his daughter and ex-wife. Jim checked out of his hotel, packed his things solemnly into the tiny trunk of his car, and sat down on a nearby bench for one last look at Murray before he drove off into the sunset. He was mulling over how much to donate to the Murray Historical Society when a shadow fell across his shoulder.

"Hi, Daddy."

A lump sprang into his throat at the sound of her voice. He scooted silently across the bench and motioned for Helena to sit down.

"Looks like you're leaving."

He nodded. "It's time for me to go, honey."

"I know." She turned to face him, appraising him with those honest brown eyes. "But I'm glad you came."

"Why?"

"I don't know. At first I wasn't. But seeing Grant almost lose his dad made me realize that we don't have time on this earth to fight."

"I know I was a terrible husband. I'm probably even a terrible man. But I always thought . . . I always hoped . . . I was a good father."

She reached over and took his hand.

"You were. You are." She smiled. "Look at me. I think I turned out all right."

"That was probably your mother's influence."

"Sure, some of it was. But you had a hand in it too." She leaned back against the bench, a thoughtful smile on her lips. "You know what I remember most about my childhood?"

Jim shook his head. He was afraid to ask.

"The picnics we used to have on the beach. You would build sand castles with me, for hours sometimes, and help me collect driftwood and shells to decorate them. You taught me how to swim." Helena looked her father in the eye. "When I think about my childhood, I remember how much you loved me. You were always there, even when things with you and Mom weren't so great."

"I tried," he said hoarsely. Visions of her as a little girl drifted through his memory: Helena twirling in circles on the sand, laughing with her arms outstretched as the ocean spray slicked her skin and the sun glinted off her hair. *Please, God, don't let me cry. Not now.* "I'm sorry, baby. I guess I've ruined your life."

"I don't think so," Helena said. "I mean, at first I did, but now . . . I don't know. It just seems like God had a plan in all this. I have a new life here. A life I really love."

"I'm glad."

They sat in comfortable silence for a moment.

"You know that I hate to leave, right? I'd stay here with you forever if I could, but I imagine it's hard on your mom."

"Yeah, Mom hasn't left the house since you arrived."

"Do you think she'll ever forgive me?"

"I don't know. Maybe someday, but I wouldn't hold your breath."

"That's OK. Making amends can be a long process." He fumbled in his pocket, then pressed a square of plastic into her palm.

"What's this?"

"It's a calling card. I'll send you a new one every month. Please use them." He ran a hand over her hair. "I don't want my baby getting away from me."

"Never," she whispered. "I love you, Daddy."

"I love you too."

EPILOGUE

JERICHO puffed out a string of panicked, staccato breaths. Emily hovered at her side, mopping her brow with a cool cloth and making soothing sounds. How had the last nine months gone so fast? Jericho's eyes rolled up toward the ceiling as another contraction mounted.

"I'm not ready for this," she gasped.

"You're ready, sweetie." Emily gripped her hand. "And you're not alone."

The hallway outside Jericho's modest hospital room was packed with eager friends and honorary aunts and uncles: Ian and Bug, Grant, Helena, Song, and Harry laughed and waited and prayed while she labored for a new life within. Emily thanked God, for what seemed the hundredth time, for her daughter and her grandchild and the fact that they were going to stay in Murray.

"Mom, I'm scared."

Emily knew how much it cost Jericho to admit that. Now was not the time to coddle her.

"It's OK, Jer. We'll get through this. You're strong, you're healthy—"

"No, not about giving birth. I'm scared of what happens after. I mean, how on earth am I going to raise this baby?" Jericho bit her lip. "He doesn't have a father. How am I going to raise this boy without a father?"

Emily brushed a lock of hair from her daughter's forehead and squeezed her hand.

"Don't worry," she said. "We'll raise him to know his heavenly Father."

Jericho suddenly smiled, a glorious revelation that broke through the clouds.

"Yes," she whispered. "We will."

Kirsten Lasinski lives in the Denver area with her husband, Richard. Together they serve in youth ministry and enjoy hiking and camping. For more information about Kirsten or her other books please visit www.kirstenlasinski.com.

Something
terrible was
coming . . .

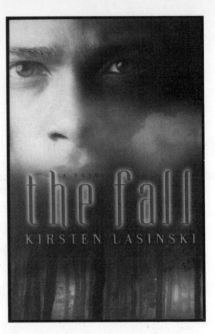

Good-guy Morris Jackson is content with his life in
the gritty urban neighborhood of Quigley Heights. A
stubbornly optimistic young man, Morris likes his
friends, enjoys his job, calls his mother every Sunday,
and tries to ignore the possibility that he may have
killed his father. But when vivid dreams of a haunt-
ingly beautiful place begin to trouble Morris's sleep,
the contrast between his idyllic visions and the rou-
tine of daily life become too much to bear.

The Fall
ISBN: 0-8024-1405-2
ISBN-13: 978-0-8024-1405-2

GUARDED TEAM

ACQUIRING EDITOR
Andy McGuire

COPY EDITOR
Michele Straubel

BACK COVER COPY
Michele Straubel

COVER DESIGN
Barb Fisher, LeVan Fisher Design

COVER PHOTO
Steve Gardner, pixelworksstudio.net,
Scott Gilchrist/Masterfile

INTERIOR DESIGN
Ragont Design

PRINTING AND BINDING
Bethany Press International

The typeface for the text of this book is
RotisSerif